LAUREL CANYON

BY

A.J. LLEWELLYN

DEDICATION

*This book is dedicated to all those who were there at Compton's Caf-
eteria in San Francisco three months before the Sunset Boulevard
riots on Saturday, November 12, 1966. Thank you for being the first
people in America to stand up for the rights for gay, transgender
and transsexual people. Thank you to all the teenagers who were the
day the musical revolution happened on Sunset. Thank you for
standing up for music.*

Thank you for taking the bully clubs.
In the name of love.

Three years before Stonewall, there were the Sunset Strip riots, where teenagers led the battle against the police. Hit with bully clubs and banned from listening to music, LA teenagers fought for acceptance, for love... And for gay rights.

Being gay was taboo in 1966. Even the hipster burger join Barney's Beanery had a sign up saying Faggots Stay Out. It had been there since 1953. LA's teenagers wanted to fight social taboos. They wanted freedom. For all.

Taris West moves to Los Angeles on November 12, 1966, the very day of the Sunset Riots. Taris, his brother, and cousin, who make up a band called Go West, find themselves in the middle of the street fight between teenagers and police. Although Taris is an eyewitness to the riot taking place on the corner of Sunset and Laurel Canyon, he is also eager to explore the mythic hills that are the home to many music legends.

Soon he's rubbing shoulders with Neil Young, Stephen Stills, Frank Zappa, Sonny and Cher, to name a few. There's also a slightly mysterious former Air Force officer named Winter, who's moved to Laurel Canyon to pursue his own musical fortune. Winter is incredible, but he also has a weirdo roommate who puts off everybody he meets. There's also something strange going on in Winter's Laurel Canyon house. Somebody keeps bumping and scraping in the middle of the night and a mural above his bed keeps getting additions as Winter and Taris sleep.

Can these two broken men find acceptance, or even love, as history evolves right in front of their eyes? Can they make music together? And what about the burning civil rights issues of the day? Can a little canyon help mend bridges across the universe?

Frank Zappa often said, "Laurel Canyon is freaky, man."

This book has been previously published. It has been edited and revised for republication.

Laurel Canyon
Copyright © 2019 A.J. Llewellyn
ISBN: 978-1-4874-2653-8
Cover art by Martine Jardin

Published by eXtasy Books Inc or
Devine Destinies, an imprint of eXtasy Books Inc

Look for us online at:
www.eXtasybooks.com or www.devinedestinies.com

"So we're the house band at the Whisky a Go-Go, and I'm sitting upstairs looking out the window, and it's complete gridlock and thousands of hippies on the street and I said, 'Wow, we're taking over.'"

John Densmore, The Doors.

"There's something happening here. What it is ain't exactly clear.
I think it's time we stop, children, what's that sound?
Everybody look what's going down."

"For What It's Worth" Buffalo Springfield, music and lyrics by Stephen Stills, written immediately after the Sunset Boulevard riots.

CHAPTER ONE

Saturday, November 12, 1966, 2 P.M.

We rolled along Sunset Boulevard that warm, sunny afternoon, marveling at not only the differences in temperature from our chilly Northern California home of Tiburon, but the fact that we'd finally made it here. Sixty-two degrees, twenty above the dreary weather we'd been having back home. Then there was the terrain. None of us had ever seen such lavish estates. We kept losing the radio signal, and I fiddled with the dial until I finally found a music station as we crawled into the outskirts of Beverly Hills.

I had the wheel of my brother Ray's rusted-out white 1959 two-door American Rambler. Neither Ray, who was sitting beside me, nor our cousin Will, who was loitering in the backseat, had any idea I'd been praying the last fifty miles. I'd been silently begging the old girl not to clap out on me before we reached Laurel Canyon.

Laurel Canyon. The ace. The apex. The nexus of our dreams.

It had been a rough trip, and the tension was so thick in the car it almost choked me, but that sign... Man oh man, we all gasped and let out our breaths when we glimpsed it.

Beverly Hills.

I gotta be honest. Even though I was against the establishment, I got a kick outta seeing the famous brown and gold sign and the big pink and green Beverly Hills Hotel. We were here! Almost in Hollywood! We were gonna make it. We were all gonna be superstars!

Traffic snarled to a complete stop.

"What gives?" Ray asked, as I gripped the wheel, coaxing the Rambler into not falling apart on me. I worked the dial once again as faint voices turned to static, filling the air. Our radio was for shit. The opening strains of the New Vaudeville Band's quirky new hit song suddenly blasted out at us. I loved *Winchester Cathedral*, even though we'd now heard it a thousand times driving down the 405 Freeway.

That song just made me want to dance.

We'd emptied out at the Sunset Boulevard exit. That had been a mess. The southern portion of the freeway was under construction, so we assumed that explained the congested traffic. But no. We'd been on Sunset for thirty-seven minutes and driven three miles.

We sang and grooved with the catchy lyrics until we got to the last line. I winced, trading glances with my brother, who also stopped singing. I turned to look over my shoulder at Will. He blew out a sigh as he ran a hand over his face. Man, I shoulda changed the station the moment I heard that song, but it was kinda hard to avoid it these days. The DJs loved it and seemed to play it every five minutes.

Will's baby hadn't left town. That was the sore point. We'd done a moonlight flit the night before, leaving notes for our parents. We'd planned our escape to freedom for months. Ray and I, being twins, were the youngest and had just celebrated our twenty-first birthdays. Jessamine and Will were older than us by two years, but she'd panicked, changing her mind at the last minute.

My cousin thumped his fist against the roof of the car. He loved that girl, but what he was really pissed about was that we were supposed to make our getaway in Jessamine's spankin' new, butter-yellow 1966 Ford Thunderbird convertible with the 8-track deck. That vehicle was her baby. And she took pride in her collection of 8-tracks. Our plan had been to drive down the coast, top down, diggin' the tunes. Instead, she never came to pick us up a little before midnight, like we'd arranged.

We'd crept over to Jessamine's house, lugging our duffle bags, guitars and amps. Will climbed the trellis to her bedroom on the second floor of her parents' home and tapped gently at her window. She came down to the front yard a few minutes later, huddled against the cold in her nightgown and flannel robe. I will never forget her fluffy purple slippers, or her tears.

"I can't do it," she said. "My father trusts me."

"What do you mean you can't do it?" Will fought to keep his voice low, but he was struggling with the West family's legendary inclination to yell. We were a family of screamers, which was groovy on stage, but kinda played havoc in our relationships.

"I have to stay. He gave me that car." She turned and looked lovingly at it in the dim light of the streetlamp near the driveway. It gave such a romantic glow to the damned vehicle. She glanced back at us. That's when I noticed the curlers in her hair. Those things took her forever to roll into her long locks, so it seemed to me she'd known all night she wasn't going to run away from home. She could have called and told us, but no. Jessamine opened her robe and pulled out a paper bag. "I got you all some presents."

She cried as she gave Will a bottle of her favorite Love's body lotion. "Wear it and think of me. I'm not going anywhere. I'll be right here."

I got her dog-eared copy of Sylvia Plath's depressing poetry, *Ariel*, that all the girls liked for some reason.

"You'll love this, Taris. You have soul," she said. I was beginning to revise my negative opinion of her on the spot.

Most mystifying of all was her giving Ray a tube of Clearasil, since he had the clearest skin of everyone I knew, but he seemed to like it. To be honest, I wasn't too unhappy she wasn't coming. She's a temperamental singer and always struck me as being high maintenance. Maybe that's why Ray was so happy with his strange gift. After all, he'd loved her first but then she'd gone after Will.

The only thing that did bother me was driving all the way from Tiberon in Ray's unpredictable car. I'd been practicing my Grammy acceptance speech since I was five years old. I was always going to say, "I came to Hollywood with two hundred dollars and my dog, Brutus. I've still got the dog." Jessamine ruined all of that. Her and her darned curlers and fluffy feet. Okay, so she wasn't a great singer, but I'd learned quickly that this had no bearing on a performer's success.

When they were together, Will thought she was great

Now, as a female singer came on the radio, we stopped talking and listened to Joan Baez's radiant cover of Bob Dylan's *It's All Over Now Baby Blue.*

"Jessamine could never sing like this," Will blurted. "She sings like she's pulling out her own fingernails."

"People say Joan is the Baby Blue in the song," I said, to change the subject. I didn't think it was fair of Will to put down Jessamine because she was so afraid of change. Most people we knew were. My own father had flipped out at the clothes I tried to wear, calling me a rebel rouser. Bell-bottom trousers, the hottest things in clothing were akin to devil worship in his mind. I knew he'd blame me for leading Ray astray.

"I heard that, too," Ray said. "They already broke up, didn't they?"

"No idea." I didn't. Anything I knew about singers' lives I read in the papers. I tried not to think about the fact I'd have to buy my own from now on. I was used to my parents paying for everything.

I wouldn't miss my dad. I already missed my German shepherd, Brutus, but he wouldn't have fit in the Rambler.

Our musical gear was jammed in the backseat alongside Will. And besides, my parents love him, too. I gulped now, realizing I was already down to a hundred and eighty-nine dollars.

On the radio, the New Vaudeville Band's sprightly brass section stopped tooting its horns. "We interrupt this program with the latest news from the Sunset Strip," an announcer said. "There is to be a peaceful demonstration at six o'clock tonight at Pandora's Box on Sunset Boulevard. Further news as it develops."

A ripple of excitement ran through the car. Pandora's Box was a hot music club where *everybody* played. The Doors, Jan and Dean, The Beach Boys, Dobie Grey and Jack DeShannon, Buffalo Springfield—

"Wonder what they're protesting?" Will asked, echoing my thoughts.

The traffic surged forward again as we inched along Sunset. *See, I'm practically a native already! I call it Sunset, just like Jim Morrison did in his newspaper interview last week!*

None of us said anything. There was something in the air. You could feel it. I looked around at the other cars on the street, and their occupants seemed to be craning forward, too, scanning for action.

"There's gotta be more news." Ray fiddled with the dial as I prayed to the god of all Ramblers not to let this one sputter and die on me. As much as I hated the car, Ray loved it.

I checked on Will through the rearview mirror. He thrust a hand through his matted blonde hair and flung himself harder against the backseat. He had the same blondish brown hair and brown eyes that Ray and I had but he'd splashed out—literally—on some peroxide, and bought himself some puka shells. Suddenly the girls were going wild for him.

Will and Ray had been fighting all the way from San Francisco, which was where we first broke down at three o'clock in the morning. It wasn't like them, but these were unusual circumstances. We'd been cooped up for fourteen hours together and we'd all started to wonder how our parents were dealing with the news of our leaving.

Every time a cop car neared us, we all flew into panic, convinced our parents had called them to haul us home. But we were adults now. They wouldn't call the cops. They'd wait until they heard from us and undoubtedly find creative ways to lure us home. For Jessamine, staying put had come at the bargain price of limitless eight tracks. And, probably, a lifetime's supply of fluffy slippers.

We'd all given up college after our third year. Our official story was that we wanted to take a year off and that we'd come home and finish our studies. It was just too hard being in a hot band in Tiburon *and* going to school.

"We're here," I said. "We did it." I swallowed. Hard. We'd been encouraged by well-meaning friends to make the break for freedom. I knew Will's parents would blame me for his break for the open road, too.

But still, we'd followed our dreams. Though they hadn't included Jessamine's defection, two flat tires, a clapped-out engine, a speeding ticket, and a gas tank running on empty, it was good. We were free.

The Beach Boys song, *Good Vibrations*, came on. Maybe it was a positive sign we wouldn't run dry.

"We need gas," Ray said, as though reading my thoughts.

There wasn't a station in sight and hadn't been one since we got off the freeway. We were all anxious, and I was afraid Will and Ray would snap at each other again, which was funny considering the astrology chart my mom had done for me a few days ago as my birthday gift. Somehow, Ray got all the glorious gifts of the universe, but my chart was full of doom and mayhem.

"Taris," she'd said, jabbing a finger at a triangle pattern dotted with illegible squiggles in the middle of what looked like a pie chart. "This is your fourth house here. You're destined to be broke always, with this trine over Saturn."

Gee, thanks Mom.

She'd turned pale. "Oh, and look here. This is why you don't have a girlfriend. You have problems in your relationships because you get moody and quarrelsome."

Quarrelsome? Me? I was the pacifist in the West family. I'd had to agree with her though, because denying it would make me seem er... quarrelsome. I couldn't tell her I didn't have a girlfriend because I was gay. My parents would have a cow if they ever knew about that. As cool as they were about some things, they had issues with homosexuality and also, race. It always shocked me the things they came out with, especially when it came to what she referred to as "queers." Long hair, music, and tie-dyed clothing were also hot button topics for them.

Running away was the only chance I had of being myself, of doing all the things I wanted without my mom saying I was selfish. That was her constant refrain.

"You'll have a chance at a good relationship when you're thirty-two," she informed me with confidence. "I don't see children in your future but maybe that's a good thing. You are, after all, the most self-absorbed person I've ever met."

It had shocked me when she said that. I didn't think it was true but as usual, just sucked up the personal insults. She and my dad had suggested hormone therapy for me when my brother was busy getting into trouble with girls. "They are doing marvelous things with shock treatment," they'd said, showing me a brochure for some hospital back East. That had been three days before Ray and I left.

He was the only one in my life, apart from my first love, Justin, who knew my secret. Ray had struggled with my sexuality. I knew that, but after a year or so, he thought it was fine. He didn't have to worry about me going after his girlfriends, unlike Will, who seemed to want anyone and anything that Ray loved. And besides, girls liked me and tended to talk to me first, which was handy for Ray who could swoop in and date them.

Ray had been as disturbed as I about the proposed shock therapy. "There's nothing wrong with you," he said. "You don't need to be fixed."

I appreciated his support and I wasn't going to wait around long enough for my parents to nag me about their proposed medical treatments. I wondered if they suspected I was gay, but I'd always been careful. I'd had one boyfriend and he was no longer around.

"Do you think they know?" Ray asked me after Mom brought the topic up again over our evening meal of Chicken à la King. It became contentious. The conversation, not the creamy casserole dish she produced with alarming frequency.

"Don't you want to be normal?" she screamed at me across the table.

I want to have at least one meal a week that's not swimming in canned soup! I went to my room plotting my escape. Ray called Will and Jessamine, not letting on the urgency of our quest, but for me, leaving was my only option. We arranged it for the following night, because things were so tense at home.

Will told me he and his mom heard my mom yelling at me from their home across the road.

"She said, 'I don't know why Sheila always picks on that boy. Taris is a fine fellow. He's a bit unusual, but his fingernails are always clean,'" Will told me.

Mom had never been one to apologize. *Sorry* was not in her vocabulary. She would apologize by being nice for days after an outburst. True to form, a few hours after she ruined dinner, she knocked on the door and brought me a slice of Tunnel of Fudge cake, the hot new dessert she and her friends were all making these days.

"You didn't finish your dinner," she said. I could see she'd been crying.

I almost melted except that she put the cake plate on the desk beside me, with a new brochure. She'd encircled the details of a program designed for 'Fever and Mental Disease.' She broke my heart right there. I took a deep breath and shoved the brochure in my drawer, trying not to think. *She believes I have a mental disease.*

Go West had things to do, shows to play, people to meet. We didn't go west, we went south, then slightly inland, east, but oh—

Suddenly, it happened. The things I'd heard about were true. We'd inched into West Hollywood and it was real! You couldn't drive for all the kids streaming along the street. Ray shrieked as hot chicks in leather shirts, cool guys in jeans—bell-bottom jeans—and love beads, ignored the lights and the honks of cars to cross the street.

A guy approached us with a bunch of flyers in his hands and slapped one on the windshield and kept moving. We all jumped from the impact.

"What is it?" Ray squinted as I reached around and plucked the flyer before it could fly away.

"It's a notice about the demonstration," I said. A grainy black and white photo of Pandora's Box topped the page. "Here, you read it aloud," I told my brother as the traffic surged forward again.

Ray turned down the radio and did as I said. "In observance of the outdated law of a ten p.m. curfew for teenagers visiting all the clubs on the Sunset Strip, there will be a peaceful protest tonight outside Pandora's Box, which is being victimized by Los Angeles Police Department and the City Council."

Will cut into his speech. "Ten p.m.? Man, are they kidding? Parties are just getting started then!"

"I know, right?" Ray continued reading. "This is an infringement of our civil rights." He looked at me. "The

9

demonstration is being organized by RAMCON, the Right of Assembly and Movement Committee. Says here they're head-quartered in the Fifth Estate Coffeehouse. Eight-two-two-six Sunset."

I didn't respond. I'd just seen Pandora's Box, and almost careened into the car in front of me as I drank in the sight of it.

Up ahead, the pink and purple club with vertical gold stripes sat in a kind of triangular island in the middle of Sunset.

"There she is!" Will yelled, pointing.

Kids were milling about the club already. I grinned from behind the wheel as I glimpsed the first protest signs. VW camper vans and motorcycles held up the flow of traffic from the Westside, but we didn't care.

"Man, I told you we were driving the wrong vehicle," Ray said. He cheered up as more pretty, longhaired girls in mini-skirts flashed peace signs at us. We flashed 'em right back.

We were dressed all wrong, too. Jeans and T-shirts. I lost count of the bell-bottom leather slacks, green wool Norfolk jackets and the headbands I saw.

Pandora's Box was literally on a dry, patchy island in the middle of Sunset. As we idled at the intersection, I noticed a street sign indicating Laurel Canyon to the left, Crescent Heights to the right.

The light turned green, but the nonstop parade of people didn't give me much chance to move. The Rambler gave a strange sort of shudder, emitted great puffs of rancid smoke, and died.

"No!" we all screamed.

It was our worst nightmare.

"Taris!" my brother yelled. "Do something!"

What the heck did he want me to do? I put the car into neutral and stepped outside. I kept the door open, one hand on the doorframe, the other on the wheel trying to steer her forward, but she was heavy.

"Help me," I yelled at Ray as I leaned my full weight against the door. He got out, Will climbing over the front seat to join us, and we pushed. It wasn't easy with all the kids milling around us. I glimpsed some pumps through the sea of people. "There's a gas station on the corner of Laurel Canyon!" I shouted to Ray. "Steer left!"

The three of us pushed the smoky vehicle up the incline toward the canyon, and suddenly the going got easier. Several guys and girls had started helping us. My dad had such disdain for hippies, yet these were the friendliest strangers I'd ever met. We got the car into the gas station. A mechanic came over to us, a grubby cloth in his hand. He waved at the putrid stream of smoke and helped us edge the car toward the back of the premises.

We stood around as he popped the hood and a fresh wave of noxious grey fumes puffed out at us.

"Congratulations. You just blew out your engine," he said.

"How much to fix it?" Ray asked with a practiced air. The poor old Rambler had a lot of miles on her and was never meant to make a journey like this.

"Fix it? This car needs a burial at sea." The mechanic stuck his foot on the front fender and propped an elbow on it as he stood over the engine for a closer look.

Ray's face turned crimson. Will and I backed away. Ray had a thing about his car, but also had a way with people. He'd been advised to junk her since the day he bought her four years ago. My dad kept saying she'd had more comebacks than Nellie Melba, who was apparently some ballerina who didn't know when to quit.

I walked over to the two payphones hugging the corner and fished a dime out of my wallet. Jessamine had procured the phone number for somebody called Fania, who lived on

Laurel Canyon, and was supposed to be able to find us a room to rent.

As I waited for the call to go through, I tried not to inhale the foul stench of cigarettes from the receiver, or the oil burn drifting past my nose from Ray's car. I looked up at Laurel Canyon. It was leafy and rustic-looking, just as everyone said. They also said the canyon gave birth to the music sound everybody said we'd fit right into.

Now we were here, I wasn't so sure. I was the lead guitarist of Go West, Ray was the drummer, and Will played bass. The realization had just sunk in that we didn't have a singer anymore. Jessamine screwed up the lyrics all the time, but she looked so hot on stage she could have sung "la la la" all night and still get rave reviews.

With the phone still ringing, I dragged my gaze in the other direction. I focused on the Lytton Savings bank building and Pandora's Box, which stood across the road from it. Lytton Savings had taken over a corner once inhabited by the apparently stunning Garden of Allah bungalows. Lytton's had a vast expanse of grass now being inhabited by groups of kids laughing and talking.

In between the moving bodies, I glimpsed a large sign on the side entrance. It read, *Friday and Saturday Open: 8.30 p.m. to 2 a.m. No Club Jackets, Sweaters or Shirts Allowed on these Premises.* A hand-painted sign on the white picket fence surrounding the structure said, *No Minimum.*

A police car cruised by, slowed, but didn't stop. The occupants didn't seem to notice the huge crowd gathering in the street. People parted to let the vehicle through. I noticed a couple of picket signs saying, *We're Your Children! Don't Destroy Us* and *Ban the Billyclub.*

Will came over to me. "You callin' that woman with the room to rent?"

I shrugged. "Yeah, but she's not answering." I hung up the receiver and retrieved my dime from the slot.

"Come and grab your gear. Ray doesn't have the money to fix the Rambler. Not that he's told the mechanic that."

I fell into step with him. "What's he going to do?" My heart sank. We needed a car. Nobody got around L.A. without one.

Will lifted his hands. "He told the mechanic he'd get the money to fix it. He's gonna leave the car here for now."

I saw the woebegone look on Ray's face as we emptied the vehicle of our belongings. I slung my guitar over my right shoulder and gripped the handles of my duffle bag. Everything seemed so much heavier than it had the night before. Ray stuck the amps that had been in the backseat into the trunk with his pared-down drum kit.

"Too heavy to carry," he said, keeping his drumsticks on hand. Where to now?" He was trying to sound okay about the loss of his wheels.

"I could use a cold drink. Maybe a sandwich," Will said.

"What about the room?" Ray asked.

"No answer," I said. "Let's grab a cup of coffee and something to eat, then we'll give her another try."

Ray heaved a sigh as he threw his duffle bag onto his shoulder. "That sounds good to me right now."

"There's a coffee shop over there." The mechanic jabbed a finger to his right.

"Thanks," Ray and I said in unison. We headed over to it. Tons of kids were draped over the wrought-iron bars out front of The 5th Estate on the next corner. Somebody had spray-painted *End Police Brutality* in black paint on the front of the building, and people stared at us as we entered the packed premises.

There was the pleasant hum of something brewing as we looked around, and it wasn't just the aroma of fresh coffee. We waited for a table, and I studied the posters on the walls. I loved seeing the colorful images of The Byrds, The Doors, Eric Burdon and The Animals, most of them autographed. I drank it all in. Better than coffee. Better than two cups even.

My dad had gone mad when we first broke the news that we planned to take off a year from college. He'd insisted we go to night school, but that was when our band, Go West, played gigs. Well, two so far, but both had been sensational. We even had a fan club. So what if we'd started it ourselves?

"You don't play," Dad had said with a snarl. "Your band just rehearses. You can keep doing that. Just go to school at night."

"Sorry, Dad. No can do," I'd responded. I loved that expression. *No can do.* I'd heard Jim Morrison say it on the radio. Dad shoved me away from him and put his hands on his hips.

"My house, my rules," he said.

Shit. Sorry, Dad. No can do.

The line for a table seemed to stretch forever. It was like a sea of leather jackets and stovepipe pants, the faint scent of patchouli oil invading the more pleasant aroma of coffee. I couldn't help thinking, *Mom would love it here.* The packed tables were filled with people putting away food like they were going to the chair. Just as we were about to give up and try someplace else, I locked eyes with a guy across the room. His hair was dark and not as long as mine—which reached my shoulders—but curled nicely below his ears. His piercing green eyes mesmerized me.

He beckoned us over to his table for four, which he was sharing with a couple of guys. A couple vacated the seats beside them. We scrambled to thread our way through the countless kids clustered around tables. When we reached the dark-haired guy, he stood and grinned at me.

"Hey, man, you're welcome to share our table." He shook my hand after I'd propped my guitar and duffle bag against the wall. "I'm Winter. James Winter, but I just go by Winter." I liked his name. Ray, Will, and I introduced ourselves. "This is Brent." He pointed to a guy with chestnut hair. He had the weirdest cut I'd ever seen, like he'd trimmed it himself with

14

his eyes closed. Brent's bushy beard needed some attention, and his T-shirt had seen cleaner days. The fearsome tattoos on his forearms were intimidating. He nodded to us and kept strumming his guitar.

Winter's other friend said nothing. His face looked familiar. He seemed older than the rest of us, with his carefully combed mop of hair and a fake fur vest. I noticed the sheriff's badge pinned to it. Although he had a huge smile on his face, there was fear in his eyes.

"This is Sonny." Winter gestured to his friend.

"Nice to meet you." Sonny shook our hands but kept glancing around. I tried to place him and wondered if he was a politician. He gave off an air of authority, but couldn't have been a real cop. The choice of the sheriff's badge struck me as off, considering the tension in the coffee shop and out on the street.

A harried-looking waitress came over to us. "What'll you have?" she asked me.

"Coffee and a ham and cheese sandwich. Please."

"Me, too," Ray echoed.

"And me." Will winked at her.

"You're easy to please." The waitress winked back at Will, who seemed to spark to life. He stared after her. Boy, he was getting over Jessamine fast.

A very pretty, serious-looking girl with dead-straight, long black hair parted down the middle, a luminous smile and a face full of pimples, joined our table.

"Hi!" she said, taking a seat on Sonny's lap. She, too, wore a fake fur vest and her black and white striped bell-bottom pants were the widest I'd ever seen.

Winter laughed. "And this is Sonny's better half, Cher."

Ah. Now I recalled him. Sonny and Cher. They'd had a big hit last year. I tried to recall the name of the song as Cher plopped a fringed, stripy purse on the tabletop. Ray kept

staring at it. I couldn't figure out why until the waitress returned with our food and distracted everybody. Cher turned
to say something to Sonny, and Winter was shouting behind
him to the people at the next table. Ray chose that moment to
drop Jessamine's tube of Clearasil into Cher's purse.

Man, it was hard to keep a straight face when he did that. I
glanced over at Brent. His eyes were closed as he strummed,
but his hand didn't seem to be touching the strings. What a
weirdo.

I picked up my sandwich but hardly had a chance to take
a bite when Winter jostled me.

"Quick!" he screamed at Sonny, leaning forward to him.
"The mayor just arrived."

Sonny jumped from his seat, almost sending his wife to the
floor. I reached to help her up, and she gave me a grateful
smile. She was lovely, and I wondered again about Sonny
wearing the sheriff's badge. The mayor, a frightened-looking
guy in a dark suit and crisp white shirt, was introduced as
Sam Yorty. I glanced at Winter, who showed clear disdain for
the mayor. He rolled his eyes as Yorty shook Sonny's hand
when Sonny reached the top of the room.

Yorty began to address the crowd. Nobody moved as he
said, "I invite you all to come to City Hall and voice your concerns."

The crowd began to mutter and groan. A few people
laughed.

"We don't wanna listen to Saigon Sam," Brent suddenly
said, the only words he'd spoken since we'd arrived.

A few people applauded. Some laughed. Winter's bright
eyes swept the room. I wondered about the Saigon Sam reference and figured I could ask Winter later on, but the mayor
now looked pained.

He held up a hand. "Please. Things are very tense right
now. Sunset Boulevard is home to some fantastic clubs and

coffee houses, but it's also the home of many residents who are the ones who asked for the nighttime curfew to be enforced. By the way, it was created in nineteen-thirty-nine, and nobody's thought to use it in decades."

"Until now," somebody muttered. I was stunned when I realized it was Will.

The crowd grew restless, so Mayor Yorty yelled to be heard over them. "They're working people, and they need their sleep. I understand your concerns about the possible closure of Pandora's Box, but I urge you all not to resort to violence."

As speeches went, it wasn't impressive.

Ray leaned into me. "Trust us to come out here just when things are about to explode. I don't want to riot. I just want to make music, man."

"Just be cool tonight, okay?" Sonny asked the crowd. "Just be cool."

I stared at him. Most of the people in the coffee shop looked furious. Some shouted. Others shook their heads. The mayor didn't stay long. He took off, and Sonny looked across at our table. As if pulling an invisible string, he seemed to spur his wife into action.

Cher picked up her purse and gave us all a finger wave and rushed to join Sonny.

"He wants to be mayor one day," Winter informed me. I glanced at him. There was something deeply disturbing yet utterly hypnotic about the way he looked at me. It was odd that in that moment, a shiver of something like pleasure ran through me at the same moment I remembered the name of Sonny and Cher's hit song.

Baby Don't Go.

CHAPTER TWO

The waitress at The 5th Estate offered to look after our bags and instruments when we paid for our food and said we wanted to check out the action on Sunset. We stowed our things in a back storeroom, but I never left my guitar anywhere. I slung it over my shoulder as we hit the street. I loved seeing Schwab's Pharmacy in all its glory. We peered through the windows, and Ray made a crack about how we might get discovered.

"We need to sit on the soda fountain stools," he said. "Hey, it worked for Lana Turner."

"That was a phony story," Winter said.

I didn't say anything. I'd just seen a waitress opening a can of fruit salad and dumping it onto a plate of lettuce, then serving it to a customer. It was just like the kind of food my mom made.

Still, there were other legends deeply ingrained that were hard to let go of, such as songwriter Harold Arlen writing the beautiful *Over the Rainbow* at a small table just inside the door, by the light of the drugstore's neon sign.

"I'd like to try writing a song in there," Ray announced, "But I'm all out of inspiration right now." The day grew cooler as we strolled west along Sunset. I tried to reach Fania again from one of the phone booths outside Lytton Savings. The call rang out once again, and when I emerged, the others were clustered around a glass case under a cement dome. I stuck my head around Ray's shoulder to see what they were looking at and was surprised to find it was a model replica of the Garden of Allah, which had stood here only a few years ago, knocked down only to be replaced by the ugly bank building. I looked over at the colorful, vibrant Pandora's Box. Now they wanted to get rid of that unique piece of history, too.

We kept walking along the boulevard. The Plush Pup coffee shop with its bright green umbrellas out front bore signs forbidding motorcycle riders to enter the premises. *Do not park out front or in the driveways!* A second sign underneath it read, *We will not serve motorcyclists!*

Both The Plush Pup and The Whisky a Go-Go across the road had huge billboards above them advertising The Frontier Hotel in Las Vegas. *Put Yourself in our Place!*

"The acting crowd and older-type singers are heading to Vegas," Winter told me. Rock music is taking over the Strip."

I grinned. "I hope to be part of the revolution."

"You're a guitarist. I can see that. What's the name of your band?"

"Go West."

"All Points West," Ray corrected me. He'd been walking ahead of us with Will. This was something he and Will had been arguing about on the drive down. Will had wanted to change the band's name. Ray had resisted. Now we were suddenly All Points West. When were they going to mention that to me?

Cream was the house band, according to the huge stenciled sign above the entrance. In much smaller letters near the bottom were the words, *Things to Come.*

"I wonder if that means the rally tonight," I said.

"Nah, bird brain. They're a band. They've got a new song out. Forget what it's called," Ray responded. How did he know this? I hated when he had even the tiniest piece of information that I didn't.

"Sweetgina," came a gravelly voice from behind us. Out of

nowhere, Brent, the weird guy with the strange haircut appeared. He stared across at the Whisky. "It's a cool song, and I like Cream all right too, but, man, that place was happenin' when The Doors was the house band. They got fired for saying fuck on stage back in August."

"They're playin' tonight," somebody else said. "It's supposed to distract the kids from throwing punches at the fuzz."

"I thought they were playing in New York this month," Ray said. Man! Where did he learn this stuff?

Brent rubbed his hands together. "Let's hope they're here for old time's sake and let' hope they make trouble!" He fell into step with us as we passed the Jay Ward studios with a spinning Rocky and Bullwinkle out front. Bullwinkle was purple, which surprised me, but then I'd only seen him in black and white on TV. Right next door was a dress boutique called Belinda.

"See ya," said Brent, who should have checked out some new threads. He walked down the street, muttering to himself.

The rest of us walked inside. Only Ray and Will seemed interested in the skinny sales assistant with the heavy makeup and gold mini-skirt. She kept giggling, and they kept flirting. Winter and I checked out the vinyl. There was a 45 single of Bob Candee's hit, *You Got It, (I Want It).* I loved that song. It had been a hit a few years ago. I almost bought it, but until I had a job and knew I had income, I had to watch my pennies. I wrestled with my desire for the record. It was only forty-nine cents. The devil on my shoulder urged me to buy it. The angel on the other shoulder reminded me I had no record player. I'd left it at home, along with my comfortable bed. And my sweet dog.

I swallowed over the sudden well of emotion and bought the record.

Winter was looking at the men's fashions. A rather

foppish-looking guy rang up my purchase on an old gold cash register. I slipped the record into a side pocket of my soft guitar case and slung it over my shoulder once again. Green Velvet was explaining to Ray that Belinda, for whom the store was named, was a designer, and that she had a huge clientele.

"If you're looking for a part-time job, we're looking to hire," he said. I couldn't take my eyes off the guy. He wore a ruffled white shirt with a green velvet jacket.

I almost asked if I could apply for the job when I caught a sign next to the dressing room. *No Camel Waterin', Bra Swaping, (somebody couldn't spell), Nellie Trading, Batmobile Parkin', Bad Trips, Phony Checks, Help Wanted.*

Nellie Trading. Was that a derogatory term for gay men? I had no intention of picking up guys here. I just needed a job. I caught Winter's gaze. He inclined his head toward the front door, and we went outside.

"Could you believe that sign?" he asked me.

I bit my lip. "No."

"You know, I thought I'd heard every nasty term for gay men, but Nellies. Man. We can't escape condemnation." He flicked a gaze at me. "You *are* gay, right?"

I nodded. I'd spent so much time being quiet on the subject of my sexuality that it felt strange to be able to respond. Winter's intense scrutiny left me feeling uncomfortable. I covered the awkward silence between us with a question.

"Why did Brent call Mr. Yorty 'Saigon Sam' back at the coffee shop?"

"Yorty went to Vietnam to support the American troops. He's been dubbed Saigon Sam by his opponents ever since." He shook the hair from his eyes. "What gets me is that he talks about the *possible* closure of Pandora's Box. It's not a possibility. What all the kids don't seem to realize, this isn't a protest march tonight. It's a funeral for the club."

The words hung between us. Ray came out of the store. "Hey, Taris, you got the phone number for that lady? They're letting us use the phone for free." I dug the slip of paper out of my pocket and handed it over, making a mental note to get it back from him. Ray had a habit of losing everything.

"Who are you trying to call?" Winter asked me.

"A woman who supposedly has a room to rent."

"What's her name?"

"Fania," I said.

"Oh, I know her. She owns most of the houses up on Laurel Canyon. She can probably find you something." He paused. "You just got into town?"

"Yep." I sighed, thinking about our disastrous trip.

"Don't worry," Winter said. "You'll find something."

I nodded. I was more worried about how we'd fix Ray's Rambler.

My brother was taking an awfully long time in the store. We walked back in, and he was having an animated phone conversation with somebody, but quickly hung up when he saw me.

"She's not there. No answer," he said.

"But you were talking to someone."

He shrugged. "Dad. I let him know we were okay." He pulled a face. "He's blaming you for leading me astray."

"Really," I deadpanned.

"Yeah." Ray grinned. "He called you a rabble-rouser."

Oh, nice. I retrieved the paper from him and pocketed it again. We headed back toward Pandora's Box and passed numerous record stores. I lost count there were so many. We walked past the club, all the way to the corner of Sunset and Vine. There was Wallich's, a massive record store, which we entered and drooled over the contents, and I walked across the road to the Brown Derby. It really was shaped like a brown derby hat like I'd seen on *I Love Lucy.*

We walked back up Sunset. It wasn't easy with the crush of people moving along with us. More record stores. Record

Paradise, Phil Harris Records, and somebody had spray-painted Bob Candee's name on a wall near a copy store that boasted a penny a page for Xerox copies. We crossed back again, passing Gazzari's supper club, the Classic Cat topless dance club, where my brother and cousin tried peering through the windows for naked girls.

At Joe Veltri and Steve Holmes Hair-a-Delic, I looked inside and saw that strange Brent guy wielding a pair of scissors on somebody's head and made a mental note to stay away from him.

Crossing back to Pandora's Box, the street was now thick with teens. I was also stunned to see so many faces I'd coveted from TV shows like *Shindig!*

I recognized the host, Jimmy O'Neill, and learned he was one of the club's owners. He addressed the crowd with a megaphone, but there was so much going on, I didn't hear a word he said. Demonstrators carried signs that said, *Stop Blue Fascism!*, *Abolish the Curfew*, and *Free the Strip, and Give Us Back Our Streets*.

We stood close to the club, and for about an hour, everything seemed pretty mellow. Most of the assembled demonstrators were clean-cut students, keen to protect their right to see their favorite bands perform. A few people strummed guitars, but the mood turned tense. I'd always thought Ray's and my struggle with our parents was a personal one. I was shocked that it was such a big issue with so many people that they were taking it to the streets.

I listened to many conversations sharing this same sentiment. The occasional motorcycle cop wheeled through—slowly—creating more tension, but nobody was acting crazy. I spotted Brent darting in and out of the crowd and focused my attention on the people around us.

Suddenly, things seemed to be happening fast. Hundreds, maybe about a thousand people had showed up. Everywhere

I looked was somebody I recalled as a performer. Frank Zappa talked earnestly to Jim Morrison. Where the hell was my camera? Musicians David Crosby, Graham Nash, and Stephen Stills milled about chatting with people.

"Nice guitar case," Graham Nash said to me. I almost fell over with shock that he actually spoke to me. I did have a great guitar case with stickers and patches from music clubs all over the world. My dad, an Army sergeant, had been stationed overseas for many assignments, and always brought me back something.

It was still early, and I lost sight of Winter. I had no idea where he'd gone, but Ray and Will had been invited over to Ben Frank's for French fries with a few musicians. Ray always did make friends quickly. I glanced around for Winter, but we got pushed around, and there were so many people, I gave up the hunt. Shame really, I liked his green eyes.

We were all hungry by now, and Ben Frank's turned out to be a diner on the Strip. Somebody handed me a piece of napkin with some fries in it and I ate, standing against a lamppost. All that walking had helped me whip up an appetite. The crowds were pouring onto the Strip as the neighborhood got dark. Night lights began popping up, and Ray tapped my shoulder.

"I got this." He indicated the fries. About a half-hour later, we made our way back to the club. Motorcycle cops were there, all wearing helmets. We couldn't get near the club, there were so many people jammed on the little island on which it had been built.

To be honest, I got worried seeing all those men in blue. They weren't playing.

I had no idea why we were here. We'd just pulled into town. This wasn't our fight... yet.

"Look," Will said in my ear and pointed out the actor Jack Nicholson. I'd seen him in a couple of horror movies and *The*

Andy Griffith Show. He came with movie star Henry Fonda's son, Peter Fonda. They stood near us, and I overheard Jack telling some other guy that he was writing a movie for Peter to star in with some actor called Dennis Hopper.

Sonny and Cher were back and waved to the crowd from the steps of Pandora's Box. Ray, Will, and I, and a host of others jumped up and down, waving back, but I lost sight of the couple again as the crowd surged forward. Everybody was trying to get closer to Pandora's Box. Everywhere I looked, others seemed to be trying to stand back and observe.

The rally began peacefully. Word went around that the protestors should sit on the ground of the Strip, blocking traffic. My brother dragged me down with him. All I could think was that I'd never sat in the middle of the road in my life. I could feel the rumble of traffic on the bitumen underneath my ass and was petrified somebody would plow through the crowd. Cars were honking, people shouting.

Then everyone held hands. For one small moment, it seemed so powerful. One of the guys outside Pandora's Box shouted over the cacophony of car horns.

"What do we want?"

"Freedom!" the street people shouted back.

"When do we want it?"

"Now!"

This mantra continued, and Ray, Will, and I joined in. We all began singing, "We Shall Not Be Moved."

People jumped to their feet, and the different pockets of protestors started to march. Vehicles kept trying to move through the crowd. The police did nothing to stop them. A few kids were so upset they pounded a VW Beetle that tried to drive through the protestors.

They thumped and rocked the vehicle as it kept moving forward. It suddenly became frightening. I noticed young men running off with their girlfriends, trying to hustle them out of harm's way. A young girl dashed past me, a puppy in her arms. She looked terrified.

A news crew with massive cameras was filming everything. My first thought was, *I hope my dad doesn't see this.*

"It's almost ten o'clock," somebody said. The police advanced, many of them wearing helmets. I watched as the police invaded the open doors of Pandora's Box. They dragged out obvious offenders of the curfew and roughly shoved them, faces against the outside walls of the club, cuffing their hands behind their backs.

This sent up a cry of alarm among the crowd.

Then, *boom!*

The terrible sound of two vehicles colliding pierced the already chaotic scene. I lurched forward thanks to the crush of the crowd. A car full of off-duty marines had gotten into a fender-bender with the VW.

The marines got out of their vehicle, and one of them punched the driver of the VW. From that moment, the fight was on. Ray, Will, and I backed away, edging toward Laurel Canyon. We managed to get out of the line of attack as police and sheriffs' deputies appeared in long lines. Armed with rifles, they marched as one, pushing back at the yelling crowd, ordering everyone to leave, but some of the protestors went berserk.

Police arrested one protestor who'd been using his guitar to hit the marines. Another group attacked a city bus until the passengers and driver got out.

I watched in horror as the protestors knocked out the windows, dented the roof with an uprooted street sign, and shoved broken bottles into the tires.

Peter Fonda was handcuffed, but Jack Nicholson took off as the fighting intensified. He disappeared up the canyon as sirens sounded and the cops began rounding up protestors. I turned to say something to Ray and Will, but they'd gone. I looked for them everywhere.

I couldn't believe how out of control things got, so fast. I glimpsed my brother over at the gas station, and it took me several minutes to make my way over to him. He said something to me, but I couldn't hear him over the sounds of sirens and people's screams. I tried to absorb it all, the terror out of something that started so great. I'd never experienced anything like it.

"The protestors didn't start that fight," Will said, "But I bet we all get blamed for it."

We walked over to Ray's car. It was still sitting there, but it had a few dings on it. Crashed soda bottles littered the ground. The gas station was closed. I checked my watch. It was eleven-fifteen, so it made sense, but with the demonstration that had just gone haywire, I probably would have stuck around to make sure my business wasn't damaged.

Smashed glass lay everywhere.

"Wow. This really got out of hand," Ray said, as a bottle flew right over his head. The guys hastily removed their music gear from the trunk. We headed over to The 5th Estate and retrieved our bags. The place was crowded, and the same waitress was working, looking absolutely exhausted. People weren't throwing things or screaming. Most seemed to be looking for refuge, nursing cups of coffee.

"We're not all lunatics," one snooty girl told Ray when he asked if she'd been part of the protest. I spotted Winter at the same table he'd been at earlier. He raised a hand in recognition.

"I suppose we should try calling Fania again," I said. "I don't know about you, but I'm beat."

Will and Ray exchanged looks.

"What?" I asked, switching my duffle from one hand to another. Outside, a fresh squeal of sirens made me shiver.

"We're leaving," Ray said.

"What?" I asked again, this time, incredulous. "What do you mean you're leaving?"

"We're headin' back home. Dad's pickin' us up at the Beverly Hills Hotel. You wanna come with us?"

"Come with you?" I gaped at him and glanced at Will. "How did this happen?"

"L.A.'s terrible," Will said.

"No, it's not. We just got here." I couldn't believe they were going back home.

"We called home this afternoon, remember? Dad left right there and then. We told them about the riot. They said not to get involved." Ray suddenly turned beet red. "Dad promised me a new car."

I stifled a groan. Man, oh man. He was so easily bought.

When I didn't respond, Ray went on. "We're keeping the name All Points West. And the songs. I was the one who wrote 'em anyway."

I opened my mouth, but my brain had gone blank.

"Anything wrong?" Winter asked, coming over to us. The look of concern on his face warmed me, even as my heart shattered.

"Ray and Will are going back home." I was still trying to process the news.

"The mechanic wants three hundred and forty bucks for the engine and two new tires." Ray handed me the keys. I'd never known him to be so decisive. Or cold. Dad must have promised him one hell of a set of wheels. "If you can scrape that together, the Rambler's yours. I already talked to him. He'll let you make payments." He looked at me, then squeezed my shoulder. "Sorry, Taris. I'm not cut out to be a rabble-rouser."

"Neither am I." Will handed me the bottle of Love's lotion that Jessamine had given him. "I gotta go, man. I just found out this afternoon that Jess is pregnant. It's a heavy scene back home."

"Wow." That shocked me. I hugged them both. I was all alone. So far, my Grammy acceptance speech had gone horribly wrong.

"Bummer," Winter said. "Good luck, guys."

Ray and Will looked at me. I knew my twin all too well. He wanted me to go with them, but I wanted this. The sirens. The music.

I wanted Laurel Canyon.

"You can come and crash at my pad tonight," Winter said. "Tomorrow, we'll find you someplace else to stay."

"Cool," I said, wondering where I'd plucked up the courage to say it. "Thanks."

My brother hugged me again, whispering, "I miss you already."

I nodded. "Me, too." And just like that, he and Will walked away from the dreams we'd shared, the music we'd made, and the struggle to get here.

At least I still had one hundred and eighty-five dollars and forty cents.

CHAPTER THREE

I got my first real look at Laurel Canyon as Winter and I made our way there a few minutes later. It wasn't much to look at, beyond a few motorcycle riders heading down from the opposite direction. We passed Hollywood Boulevard. Dang. I hadn't even had a chance to explore that yet.

As we progressed up the steep incline, the sounds of the riot seemed very far away. A long, high cement wall on the left turned out to be the buttressing wall of a brown, cemented mansion. Ahead of that, a few modest bungalows and cabins were crammed between faded mansions set far back from the narrow, twisty road. The silence, as we plunged farther up the mountain road, was eerie. I was used to wilderness, having spent my whole life in Tiburon, but whereas my hometown was lush due to constant rainfall, Laurel Canyon looked dry. One stray match and the whole place would go up in smoke.

A sign on our left echoed my first impressions. It was a drawing of a cigarette with the words, *No Smoking in the canyon.* That actually made me laugh. I could smell reefer on the air as we moved. The higher we climbed, the chillier the air grew. I was cold, in spite of the exercise. I realized I was also hungry and tried to block the thought of how I'd spent my last night at home, but it was impossible. I'd spent the time eating my mom's homemade tomato soup and grilled cheese sandwiches, listening to The Mamas and the Papas on my birthday gift of a new GE Solid State stereo with massive speakers.

It sure beat what I had been using. My grandma's 1959

Magnavox Continental Console Stereo was the one thing she'd left me. She'd barely used it. After she died, my dad gave it to me. Inside the cabinet portion, I discovered her record stash. Grandma was a secret groover. There were albums by Bobby Darin, Dion and the Belmonts, and even Skip and Flip. The sound from it was okay, but nothing like my new system. Man, that was incredible. It had been almost as hard to leave that thing behind as it had been leaving Brutus. I'd promised the dog I'd come back for him, and I would.

I took a deep breath and took in my surroundings as we walked. Some of the big houses tucked away behind tall cedar trees and overgrown vines looked like fairy castles lit up in the night. I wondered who lived in them. They looked like they had been left over from the days when it was a secluded, semi-rural retreat for Hollywood's silent movie stars.

Although the canyon's dirt-brown hills rose above Hollywood Boulevard, some of the spidery side streets were unpaved, giving the place a rural, backwoods feel.

As we passed a street to our right called Mount Olympus, a pair of scrawny-looking coyotes strolled down from it, their heads hung low. They avoided eye contact with us. I was completely freaked out, but Winter said they lived up here and nobody let their pets out of their homes after four o'clock in the afternoon.

"Letting them stay out is like ringing a dinner bell," he said.

"Are you a musician?" I asked, changing the subject. I loved animals, and it pained me to see the starving coyotes and to think of them munching on family cats and dogs.

He grinned. "No. I'm a bartender." When I didn't respond, he said, "I'm a singer and songwriter, but I got here a year ago, and I make my living as a bartender. I'm just keeping it real by saying so."

"I think that's so cool. Do you like that work?"

He shrugged. "It's not bad, and I've made a lot of connections. I get to audition for some pretty cool folk, and I keep writing songs. I work at The Troubadour."

"Oh, I know about that place. I can't wait to go there."

He looked at me. "If you're looking for part-time work it's a great place. Tips are good. The bands are great." He gulped in a deep breath. "I came down from Oregon. Hood River, to be exact. I thought I'd come here and take the place by storm. I even had my Grammy speech prepared." He laughed, the sound ringing out loudly in the canyon night air.

Oh, brother. He'd just pulled the wool away from my eyes. I gulped. "I sorta had one, too."

He gave me a sympathetic look. We kept climbing. At the corner of a street called Kirkwood, he gestured to the left. "This is it."

To our right was a place called the Canyon Country Store.

"First thing in the morning, you can check out the community notice board," Winter said. "If anyone has a room to rent, they'll probably post a note on there."

"Okay, cool. Thanks." I was saying that a lot today.

We turned left at Kirkwood and walked up the tiny road. Vines and massive trees hugged the narrow path. I saw cars parked on both sides and wondered how two cars could fit on the road at the same time.

"They can't," Winter said, when I asked. "They are usually polite, the drivers around here. They'll let each other pass." We kept climbing until we reached the first house on the right, about a half-mile up the canyon. The paved road gave out to hard-packed dirt, but I could see that cars were still parked farther up there.

"Home sweet home." Winter gave me a warm smile. He walked up a set of weathered wooden stairs to what looked like a ranch house. A massive wooden deck jutted over the first floor. Lights and the sound of laughter indicated life beyond starving coyotes.

Winter pushed open the slightly warped front door, which opened immediately to a dimly lit living room. Sofas lined the walls. They looked so inviting after the long day I'd had. A fire burned in the fireplace, giving the room a tantalizing, roasty smell. A long, flat coffee table dominated the scene. I loved seeing all the music magazines tossed over the top of it. My mom would never let us leave anything on her coffee table.

You're not in Tiburon, anymore, Dorothy.

Some guy was sprawled on one of the sofas, strumming a guitar. He took his feet off the coffee table as soon Winter approached him.

"Hey, Jackson." Winter grinned at the guy. "Taris West, meet Jackson Browne." He glanced at me. "Jackson's a really talented singer-songwriter. You're gonna hear big things about him soon."

"Thanks, man," Jackson said.

In the far right corner, the living room opened to a dining table in an alcove. Just beyond that was the kitchen. My eyes nearly fell out of my head when I saw that creepy Brent emerging from it.

"You already met my roommate," Winter said to me. That made my heart sink.

"Just made coffee," Brent announced. "Hey, Tariff."

"Taris." Brent clearly disliked me as much as I disliked him.

"Cool guitar case." Jackson laid down his and moved over to me. Graham Nash had said the same thing. "Wanna jam?"

I hesitated, but Winter said, "Go ahead."

Placing my duffle bag against the wall, I opened my guitar case. The paper sleeve of the record I'd bought earlier in the day crackled in the zippered pocket as though reminding me it was still there.

"You've got a Gibson Dove!" Jackson came over and took hold of my guitar with reverent fingers. I glanced over at Brent. He was standing in the corner watching us, rapidly stuffing something from a blue dinner plate into his mouth with his fingers. I was certain I smelled scrambled eggs, and suddenly I was starving.

"Love the solid maple back and sides instead of the usual mahogany." Jackson turned the instrument over in his hands. "Double parallelogram fingerboard inlays. Nice. Love the two doves on the bridge, and the dove on the pickguard." He peered closer at them. Are they mother of pearl?"

"Yep."

"I love those doves."

"So do I." I grinned at him as he returned my guitar.

"You sure picked a good one," he said, returning to his own guitar.

No need for him to know my parents had chosen the guitar and given it to me for my twentieth birthday last year. I thought with a pang about my stereo, sitting at home, silent. I wondered if Dad, Ray, and Will had left for Tiburon yet. I brushed the thought aside as Jackson plucked out a cord on his guitar. "What tunes do you know?"

It was an odd moment. I felt as though I had to perform, that I would be judged on how I handled this impromptu jam.

"Go ahead," Jackson said. "Pick a song. Who do you like?"

I shrugged. "I listen to the radio a lot. I can play a lot of songs by ear. I like Simon and Garfunkle."

"Which song?"

"I am a Rock."

"I love that song," Winter said. He picked up a guitar that had been standing against the wall. He looked at Brent. "Get your drums."

Brent glared at him. "I'm eating!"

"Food can wait. Let's jam." Winter gave him a look that

sent Brent scurrying across the room. He brushed past me. I got a distinct whiff of reefer, not that I cared, but it seemed to explain a lot. The guy was freaky. He went out of the living room and opened a door to what looked like a bedroom. A very untidy one. He caught my gaze as he turned on the light and slammed the door.

Winter shook his head. He glanced at Jackson.

Sitting back on the sofa, Jackson played the opening strains of the song. I sat opposite him, mesmerized by his voice. He really was good. I joined in the lyric, then Winter chimed in on his guitar. The three of us sounded pretty good.

I strummed with Jackson, digging the harmonies as the three of us sang.

Suddenly, I really missed Brutus. The truth was, this song really spoke to me. Justin, the first and only man I'd loved, had enlisted and gone to Vietnam. I knew he'd done it to get away from his abusive dad. He said he could deal with the Viet Cong better than he could his father's boots and stinging leather strap, but he went missing in action a few months into his tour of duty. His family had been notified of his disappearance, but I heard the news only after they had made arrangements for a memorial service in Marin County. I had no rights as his boyfriend, his secret one at that. I'd shut myself in my room with my dog and played the radio and records constantly.

I'd suffered in silence as so many gay men have before me.

Planning the move had kept me alive. Justin and I had always talked about it, and I wondered now if he'd survived if he would have gone through with it.

Winter, Jackson, and I, sang our hearts out, passionately belting out the chorus.

We finished the song, Brent back in the living room now with his drums. Bongo drums. He began playing them. Winter joined in with a guitar riff. Suddenly Brent stopped playing.

"I'm tired. Turning in. Keep the noise down, will ya?" He got up and left the room.

Jackson laughed when the bedroom door closed. "You weren't kidding about him." He shook his head, running his fingers along the guitar fret. He looked at me. "Have you heard *Pet Sounds* yet?"

I craned my head toward the window. "No—"

Jackson laughed again. "I mean the album." His gaze was so intense, but I had no idea what he was talking about.

"Not yet," I said.

"I had to listen to it a few times until I finally understood what the hell was going on. Now, of course, I realize Brian Wilson is a genius. Years from now it will be recognized as a work of art."

"I'll grab a listen," I said. *Grab a listen? Who talks like that? What's wrong with me?*

"You want to stay the night?" Winter asked. "Taris is crashing on one of the sofas. You can have the other. They're pretty damned comfy."

Jackson hesitated. The last ember of the fire went out, as though signaling a time for movement.

"Naw, thanks. I'm staying with friends. I s'pose I ought to get back there." He stood, picked up his guitar, and gave me a smile. "Nice meeting you. Next time, you'll have to play me one of your original songs."

"I don't have any." I stroked the dove on the fret. "My brother wrote all our songs." I took a deep breath. "I'm not really a songwriter, but I respect the craft. I'd like to hear some of your music."

Jackson pointed at me. "Next time, you will." He exchanged a swift hug with Winter. At the front door, I heard him say in a low voice, "I can't believe you let that freakozoid Brent move in. Lock your bedroom door."

"Aw, he's not that bad. And there are no locks."

"Sleep with your eyes open then. I don't trust that guy."

Jackson slipped out of the house and into the night. Winter turned to me. "You wanna sleep in my room? The bed's warm and cozy." He must have sensed my reticence. "We don't have to do anything."

"Famous last words," I quipped.

"Cute as you are, I think I can keep my hands off you." He grinned at me.

He thought I was cute? "Okay," I said. The world seemed to be unfurling like a giant palm frond. All the time I'd known Justin we'd never spent even an hour in bed together. We'd been too afraid of getting caught. I could now sleep in a man's bed if I wanted. I could play my guitar and leave music magazines lying around.

"It's much warmer in my room," Winter coaxed. Not that I needed it. I liked the guy and looked forward to some rest. His place was so cool, except for his weird roommate, but hopefully, Brent wouldn't crash into the bedroom anytime soon.

With a jolt, I remembered that I had to find a place to stay in the morning.

"Come on, goofy guy." Winter beckoned me. I followed, taking my guitar and duffle bag with me.

Once we'd left the warmth of the living room, the house was freezing. I'd had no idea it could get so cold in L.A. I'd always thought of it as being the land of perpetual sunshine.

Winter's room was a lot more orderly than what I'd seen of Brent's. I heard an odd sound of footsteps coming from his room. He seemed to be dragging something. A chair? He kept walking back and forth.

"What's he doing?" I whispered, as Winter took my stuff and placed it on his bureau.

"No idea. He moved in two days ago, and this is what he does." He paused to listen. "Sounds like he's dragging a body across the floor, doesn't it?"

I shivered. "Yeah." After a beat, I said, "Is that a chair scraping against the floor?"

"You know, I thought that, but I've been in his room when he's in the shower, and there's no chair. No trunk or chest. Nothing that he could be dragging across the floor like that."

"How... weird."

"Yeah." He had distracted me so much I hadn't even realized he was undressing me. He had my T-shirt off and had begun unbuttoning my fly.

"You're cold. Let me get you into bed." He pushed me against the big, bouncy mattress, and I stifled wild laughter. As I lay on my back staring at his ceiling, I saw paintings of mermaids and other sea creatures swimming toward the light fixture dangling from it.

"Did you paint that?"

"No. Last guy did. There's artwork in the bathroom and kitchen, too."

Scrape, scrape. Stomp, stomp.

I tried to ignore the sounds as Winter removed my shoes and dragged my jeans down past my feet. I had a mighty boner inside my tighty whities, and I was suddenly mortified. Justin had always freaked when I got hard around him. He'd been so petrified of discovery that even kissing had been forbidden. I closed my eyes as Winter cupped my cock and balls with a warm hand.

When I opened my eyes again, he had a lusty look in his eyes as he slipped his fingers through the leg hole of my underpants. My body shook at the impact of his gentle touch. I held my breath, looking up at the merman reaching across the ceiling for the mermaid. His tail was even more magnificent than hers. He also had the biggest cock I had ever seen. Suddenly, Winter's fingers had made contact with my own cock. He touched the head with reverent fingers, gripping, encircling, stroking. He knelt beside me, still fully clothed. His bristled chin rubbed against my thigh. It felt good. He roamed deeper in my underpants and grabbed my balls, holding them in his palm as though feeling their weight.

He moved back to my cock, strumming his fingers down my shaft. He tugged gently at my pubic hair nestled at the groan, and it was oddly erotic. I lay there stifling a nonstop groan, silently begging him to take me in his mouth, then feeling like a total whore. I stared up at the mermaid. A naked chick with a tail shouldn't have had me hard, but she did. The passion she and the merman felt for each other was so compelling. They yearned for the touch, the underwater embrace. I arched my body up to Winter's face, but he lifted his head.

"I'm breaking my promise," he said, his voice husky.

"Huh?" I shock myself from my carnal reverie. "What promise?"

"I said I could keep my hands off you." He gave me a mournful look. "And I pride myself on being a man of my word, Taris." He withdrew his hand from inside my underpants. The world suddenly went cold.

Noooo!

"So, if it's all right with you, I'll use my mouth instead. That way, I'm not breaking my promise, and we both get what we want."

I formed my lips into what I was certain was a loopy grin. He bent again to the task at hand.

Yeeeessssss!

He took the hip band of my underpants in his teeth and drew them down my groin, paused at the baseline of my cock and he looked up at me, merriment in his eyes.

Scrape, scrape. Stomp, stomp.

He stopped pulling and took his mouth from me. "Don't listen," he said. "He always stops. Eventually." Winter resumed his tugging, his bristled chin grazing my thigh and inflaming me even further. Justin had never, ever gone down on me. He said that made him gay. I have no idea what he thought kissing me on the rare occasions he allowed it, and jerking each other off made him, but —

Oh, man! My cock sprang against Winter's cheek. His tongue met my leaking head. Stars and fireworks danced behind my eyes as he began to suck in my shaft. His bristles felt both raw and totally hot against my balls as he worked on me. He closed his eyes, his lashes long and lovely against his skin. He seemed to love what he was doing. He sucked me all the way down and held his grip with a tightened mouth. His bristles rubbed once more, and it was a searing reminder I was in bed with a man. I'd dreamed of this moment for so long.

"God!" I called out. The noise next door stopped. I bit my lip as I came, sending a furious torrent down Winter's throat. He didn't move. When my head cleared and my crashing orgasm swept over me, I lay panting.

The noise next door resumed, almost making me laugh.

Winter finally released me, swallowing. "I knew you'd taste this good," he said and moved his face to mine. He kissed me. It was weird tasting my own juices on his tongue. He grabbed my still tender cock, whispering into my mouth. "Nice playing with you."

I wanted to reciprocate, but when I reached for his fly, he brushed my hand away.

"Sleep," he said. He stood, throwing off his clothes. I drank in the sight of his toned, naked body. He had a tattoo on his right shoulder. I recognized it immediately. As he crawled across the bed to pull down the blanket and sheets, I stared at the Air Force logo inked onto his right shoulder. The wings with a star in the center of it looked fresh.

"You were in the Air Force?" I asked.

He reached for me, holding me in my arms. The room suddenly felt cold. Justin had been in the Air Force, too.

"Yeah. I was released because I have a condition."

"A condition?" I stiffened.

"I'm gay. I didn't lie, but it took them two years to finally dump me."

I lay in his arms, surprised by the admission. "How did your family handle that?"

"They don't know. I was released after my commanding officer reported me. He only did it because I didn't want to sleep with him anymore."

"Oh, my God!"

He kissed the top of my head. "It's okay. I'm over it." He sat up suddenly. "I took a bullet for that guy." He pointed to his tattooed shoulder, and I noticed the small scar now.

"Through and through." He lifted his arm, and I saw a bigger scar between his pit and torso. "It got me an honorable discharge. The pension, when I'm old, will come in handy." He moved back down and snuggled me closer. I didn't resist.

I glanced up at the ceiling. "Shouldn't we turn off the light?"

It was his turn to stiffen. "I'm afraid of the dark. Do you mind?"

I shook my head, and he kissed my forehead.

"They tell me it's shell shock and it's supposed to get better over time." His bristles felt so sweet against my chin. I didn't think I'd be able to fall asleep with the lights on, but I did. Tormented for seemingly hours with memories of the drive down to L.A., I kept picturing the moments of disaster, my brother and cousin's continual fighting. I'd had to make peace between them constantly.

When had they become aligned and joined forces against me?

I'd always prided myself on being an observer. On being astute. I sure missed the boat on this one. It pained me, thinking about how much they seemed to hate me. Our lives had been good at home, just boring. I tried not to think of my mom's toasted cheese sandwiches and warm soup.

Scrape, scrape. Stomp, stomp.

Arrgh! The strange sounds from next door awakened me. I opened my eyes, and suddenly, it was daylight. The overhead light had been turned off, and Winter was gone. The space beside me felt cool. My stuff was still there on his bureau. I looked at his collection of books on the makeshift shelf of bricks and old pieces of wood beside me.

A copy of *Ariel*. Jeez. What was with that book? Did everyone love it but me?

I turned and looked straight up at the ceiling and almost fell out of the bed. There was fresh detail on the mermaid and merman scene.

No. It wasn't possible.

I had to be dreaming.

But I wasn't. I stood on the bed and looked hard up at the mural. Somebody had painted new seaweed, some starfish, and an octopus's tentacles wrapped around the leg of the merman. How weird. I reached up to touch, scared I'd be caught. My fingertip almost connected with one of the tentacles, and I held my breath. I finally touched it. I was right. I pulled my hand away and held the finger to my nose. Oil paint.

How weird. There was such detail to the octopus I wondered how somebody could have painted it whilst not directly underneath it. Who the hell had done it?

I wondered whether Winter was the artist, then remembered his fear of the dark. Did the noise from Brent's room have anything to do with his fear? The scraping sound next door started again, freaking me out. I got dressed quickly and left the bedroom.

The noise stopped as soon as I reached the hallway. I checked that my wallet was in my jeans' back pocket and closed the bedroom door. I looked around for Winter and heard some noise upstairs. A clock on the wall told me it was six a.m.

I noticed some polished wooden stairs and climbed them. When I got to the landing, I was surprised to see what looked like a recording studio in a compact room, leading to a huge sundeck that seemed to jut out over the entire house. Winter was sitting out there on a porch swing, strumming his guitar. He grinned up at me. My cock got hard watching him in nothing but underpants and cowboy boots.

He beckoned me. When I reached him, he said, "Thanks for the best night's sleep I've had in weeks." He obviously wasn't worried about anyone seeing us because he pulled me down by the neck of my T-shirt and kissed me.

Our kiss seemed to go on for weeks. I was dazed when he pulled away from me.

"Let's finish this inside, shall we?" he asked.

I think my hard cock gave him the response he required.

CHAPTER FOUR

We went back downstairs and headed to the bathroom, but the door was closed, and steam swirled in puffs around and under the ill-fitting jamb.

"Man, he always beats me to it and uses all the hot water." Winter frowned. He glanced at me. "You need to pee?"

"Badly." I'd been looking forward to sex, but I'd also hoped to take a leak. I was desperate.

"There's an outside toilet," he said. "Help yourself. I'll get the coffee started."

"Thanks." It wasn't sex, but it was a badly needed pee and hot coffee. It was a close call which I wanted more right now. I kept thinking of the speedy but amazing blow job he'd given me and couldn't stop grinning.

I let myself out of the backdoor, where I noticed a couple of cat dishes on the bottom step. I turned, and Winter was watching me.

"You have a cat?" I asked.

His face turned glum. "I did." He stared off into the over-grown garden. "Brent accidentally left her out one night. I found her collar and all four paws down the back there." He gestured, and I shuddered. The way he said *accidentally* made me wonder whether he suspected Brent's actions had been deliberate. Either way, it was creepy. Winter looked upset as he went back into the house again.

The backyard was pretty cool, with a lot of plants and trellises with thick, lush vines filling every space. Morning glories seemed to have invaded everything, including a tomato patch. The outside toilet was a wooden shack with a creaky door and foul odor once I went inside. My eyes adjusted to the poor light, but I almost gagged on the stench. Then I saw it. A bloated, dead squirrel on the toilet seat.

I backed out again and, in a total state of panic, retched in the garden. I kept thinking about the cat and stumbled on the ground. I needed to pee very badly. I made sure I was out of view of the house and opened my fly, peeing into a dry patch of weeds. I never thought I would be the kind of man to pee in a garden, but I now had an audience.

A couple, oddly, sitting in a bathtub naked in their back garden watched me.

"Good morning!" they said in unison, giving me a wave. Boy, was I embarrassed. I didn't know where to look. I stuck my cock back into my jeans and gave them a timid wave.

"Good morning," I croaked.

They raised their coffee cups to me. I could hear their laughter as I slunk into the house, cheeks on fire. The ones on my face, too.

In the kitchen, Winter handed me a cup of coffee. "No idea how you drink it. We have milk and sugar. And here, this is cool. You tried this Quaker Instant Oatmeal stuff yet? They just released it, and it's good."

"No," I said. "Sounds great." I was so hungry anything would have been perfect.

He gave me a bowl and spooned oatmeal and boiling water into it. As I sat beside him at the dining table doctoring my coffee and cereal, he searched for news on the demonstration last night.

A couple of radio stations had reports, but I was surprised at how salacious the announcer made it sound: "The Sunset Strip," he intoned, "The Neverland the mod set calls home..."

"What?" I said.

"I know." Winter shook his head. "*Mod set.* I don't even

know what that is. You were there last night. It's mostly students and musicians."

"Hundreds upon hundreds of teenagers gather there every Friday and Saturday night, like moths to a flame..."

Oh, man. I sat in numb silence as the announcer went on.

"Each weekend, they descend on the clubs that once played gentle violin music but have now been changed to watusi palaces."

Was he kidding? He made it sound like the watusi, a dance craze that had already fallen out of fashion was like illicit sex. He then went on to depict the rally as a violent outbreak, yet no real injuries were reported. There was also no mention of the marines who'd started the actual fighting.

"Los Angeles County Supervisor, Ernest Debs, today called the youths 'misguided hoodlums.' Teenagers think this is it. Where it all happens," the announcer went on. "The new music is what they're all seeking. As long as drums pound and guitars wail, sleep becomes a thing of the past and everybody makes it together."

I grimaced. "He makes it sound like some kind of sex orgy."

"Yeah, with a bit of violence thrown in the mix."

The radio announcer went on. "Thousands of angry youth gathered here last night to protest police brutality and the enforced curfew imposed on persons eighteen years and younger. Teenagers, inflamed over the curfew, Vietnam, the racial issue, fanned the flames of the already excited onlookers." Sounds of the night's events came over the air. I heard cars honking and the police directing traffic, but no angry youth.

"The only ones yelling were the cops," Winter said, echoing my thoughts. "What a shame things got out of hand. All we want is to hear music."

"I know."

"The mob became more and more agitated." The announcer's voice rose. "And then, it happened."

Even though I'd been there, I leaned forward, enthralled.

"The traffic stopped altogether. It's not sure even now who threw the first punch, or the first hit. It was not immediately evident for the next five hours who started the riot, but the mayor was forced to call the Los Angeles County Sheriff's Department to come in and quell the riot, using teargas and bully clubs to push back and break up the mob."

Tears came to my eyes as I heard the screaming and shouting in the background. The depiction was so unfair. I wondered what it was like out there today.

Ironically, the next thing we heard was The Beach Boys' *Good Vibrations*, which was running neck and neck with *Winchester Cathedral* for the top of the music charts. It was ironic because the song spoke for itself. But for the band that had recently performed at Pandora's Box, it wasn't a good vibe that the club was being targeted for closure.

Winter switched off the radio. "You finished your coffee? We should get down to the Canyon Country Store and see if we can't find you a place to rent."

My heart sank. I supposed that meant sex was out of the question. I swallowed the last of my coffee, which was difficult, considering the oatmeal was a congealed lump in my throat.

"Sure thing," I said, hoping I didn't sound as crushed and hurt as I felt. It was stupid to be disappointed. I couldn't expect him to offer me a place to stay. I gulped. What if I could stay? I took a deep breath and said, "You wouldn't have a room for me to rent, would you?"

He shook his head. "Nah, man. I wish I'd known about you before I rented to..." He jerked his thumb over his shoulder.

"I understand." I sounded cool, and I was nodding like a guy to whom this was no big deal.

"My cousin, Spencer, owns this place. He sleeps upstairs. That studio space is his." He paused. "He's up in San Francisco working with Janis Joplin right now. He's a session musician, plays guitar. She's working on a new album. He's back and forth all the time."

"Wow. I love her voice. Does he like working with her?"

"When she shows up. She's holed up in her house in Lagunitas a lot of the time, shooting heroin."

I knew Lagunitas very well. Like my hometown, it was a beautiful area of Marin County. I was a bit shocked by the blasé reference to her intravenous drug use. I could never stick a needle into my arm. Ever.

"You ready?" he asked, dropping our dishes into the sink along with the mountain of others already there. I stood near him and glimpsed his neighbors having sex in their tub.

"They waved to me when I was peeing," I said, stunned that I even made such an admission.

"And they didn't ask you to join them?"

"No." That shocked me.

"They're super cool people. He's a musician. She's a singer. They're known to enjoy ménages." He smiled, and I got the sense he got a kick out of trying to shock me.

In his room, I gathered my belongings, slipping my guitar back in its case. Oddly, I didn't hear the crackle of paper from the record sleeve and checked the pocket. Gone. Only one person could have taken it. Brent. I didn't think it was Winter.

Winter said, "Bathroom's free. Thank God." He took off, and I waited in the hallway a moment. Brent's bedroom door was open wide. He wasn't around, but I took a long look in it. No chair, nothing that he could have been scraping along the floor all night. There was also no ladder, no paints. No mural on his ceiling. Just a bunch of clothes and stuff scattered on the floor. A faint whiff of body odor emanated from the room.

I turned and headed to the living room just as Brent was

coming out of the kitchen with a bowl of food.

"You kept me up last night," he said.

I was dumbfounded. He was one to talk.

Seconds later, I was glad when Winter came out of the bathroom. It was for the best that he had no room for me. Brent was crazy, man.

We walked outside, guitars slung over our shoulders, the two of us inhaling the fresh air. The scent of eucalyptus hung low and heavy.

"Once we find you a place to stay, we should check out Sunset," he said.

"Yeah. I'd like that."

We walked along in companionable silence until we reached Laurel Canyon. A guy wearing nothing but a sarong called out to Winter from one of the cute, cabin-style houses, waving at him. Winter waved back.

It was only when we reached the front door that I realized the man was Brian Wilson of the Beach Boys, and he was very excited about something.

He herded us in like wayward sheep, and I was startled to see his living room contained nothing but sand, a piano, and a bench.

"Get your guitars out," he said over his shoulder and raced to the piano bench, squelching his toes in the sand as he belted out a cord. "I've been working on this all night."

I *loved* Brian Wilson's music. The Beach Boys were different to everybody else, and I was in awe of his epic talents. I was too shy to jam with him. *I can't jam with Brian Wilson!* I liked what he was playing, but I liked his wife's percolated coffee and hot, buttered toast even more. I ate, standing in her kitchen as Winter strummed along with Brian's animate key-pounding in the living room. I could see the floor full of sand from where I stood and couldn't help blurting, "You let him bring sand into your house?" *My mom would kill me if a grain of it found its way into her home.*

Marilyn Wilson laughed. "He needs to feel the sand to write." She gave me a sharp glance. "Have you heard *Pet Sounds*?"

I took a deep breath. "Not yet, but—"

She walked over to a neat stack of albums and handed me one. "Here. It will change your life. This is one of those rare albums where every single song is incredible."

"Thanks." I took it, determined to play it before I saw Jackson again. In the living room, Brian was still playing the same cord, and Winter stood, grooving to the music. I had a feeling Brian was higher than a dozen kites. Did he realize he was playing the same thing over and over?

My return seemed to prompt Winter into stuffing his guitar back into its case. I picked up mine, sliding my new LP in with it. I'd find a suitable hiding place for it that night. I tried not to be depressed at the thought that I wouldn't be with Winter. Last night had been a dream. A beautiful dream. Except for the banging and scraping sounds. And, oh, yeah, the phantom house painter.

Out on the street, Marilyn hugged us both. "If you ever need to call home," she whispered to me, "Come on over. And don't forget to bring your guitar."

"How does she know I'm new in town?" I asked Winter as we ambled over to the Canyon Country Store.

"Everybody knows everybody in Lauren Canyon," he said, with a wave of his hand. His manner was so breezy, it astonished me. Up ahead, the store was already buzzing. I smelled coffee on the air.

"Check out the notice board. I need to rap with a couple of people," Winter said. He moved off to a set of stairs on the other side of the store where some people were sitting around, sharing a joint. Laughter and the sickly-sweet smoke hovered over the air. Winter was talking to a guy in jeans and a thick sweater whose hair had been cut so badly I wondered if Brent was responsible for it.

I located the notice board and became dizzy with the numerous posts pinned to it. Somebody had lost a ring, another person had found a parrot. There was a house available on Wonderland Avenue for two-hundred-and eighty dollars a month. *Wonderland.* Loved the name but hated the price.

A handwritten note tucked underneath a sign for a VW for sale indicated there was a room for rent at the Log Cabin. The note said, Enquire Within. I assumed that meant the store. I unpinned the note and took it inside. Wow. Talk about a zoo. The place was packed. I recognized a couple of people from last night's rally, but everybody seemed subdued. I joined the line for the checkout and looked around. The store was a combination deli, bakery, and general grocery. By the time I reached the counter, I was hungry again.

I showed the girl on the cash register the note.

"Oh," she said, "That's the old Tom Mix log cabin house on the corner of Laurel Canyon and Lookout Mountain. You can't miss it. You're the first person who's asked me about it. That sign's been up there for two days."

"It was under another notice."

"Ah." She snapped some bright pink gum in her mouth. "There's no phone up there, but just head on up. The guys are nice and friendly. Tell them I sent you."

"And your name is?"

She looked at me and arched a brow. "Persephone." She said it like I should have known. I thanked her and moved out of the line. Now, which way was Lookout Mountain? I couldn't recall having passed it last night so it must have been farther up the mountain

Outside, Winter approached me. He looked excited.

"Did you find something?"

"A room up at the log cabin house on the corner of Lookout Mountain."

"I know the place. Couple of actors and a writer live there. Come on, David Crosby's invited me up to his house. The log cabin's on the way."

"David Crosby? *The* David Crosby from The Byrds?"

"Yeah. He's just a human being, Taris."

"To you, maybe. Man. You know the coolest people."

We rolled up to a house teeming with people. David Crosby came out, a weird hat on his head, guitar in hand. He gave us a wave. "Come on. Let's book!" he shouted.

A bunch of us piled into his Mustang. Winter sat in front with David, who was smoking a joint. The vehicle smelled strongly of reefer. Maybe the contact high would do me good. Make me relax. I was so anxious now I had a headache. With a pang, I thought of my family. It had only been a day and a half since I'd seen my parents, but it felt longer.

The Mustang had seen better days, better years even. But still, I would have ridden a rickshaw, with me at the helm to be near the amazingly talented David Crosby. He was the guitarist in The Byrds. I'd seen a billboard for them on Sunset. I'd read an article in a magazine saying the band members were having problems, but I loved their music. I hoped to see him performing soon.

"Yo. You in the back seat."

I broke out of my reverie. David Crosby was talking to me.

"This is you." He jerked a thumb to the left. I could hardly see for all the smoke in the car.

"Thanks," I said, working hard not to cough.

Winter turned to me. "Meet me at the Canyon Country Store at two."

"Okay," I said, grateful for the fact he hadn't completely dismissed me. I got out of the car. David drove off before I'd even closed the door. One of the other guys sitting in back reached out and closed it.

I stood for a moment in the middle of the road and stared

at the massive house on the corner of Lookout Mountain. It wasn't a cabin. It was a gigantic wooden mansion with a brick chimney and what looked like a huge pond in front. It was beautiful. I crossed the road and entered the property. It smelled divinely of eucalyptus and pine. There were lights on inside the house, and I wondered if the occupants were home or if they had never made it there last night. I knocked on the front door and waited.

A guy eventually came, after yelling, "Hang on," from somewhere deep inside the house. He opened the door and looked at me.

"Who you?"

"Persephone sent me."

"That's an unusual name."

I smiled. "I'm Taris West."

"Ah. I like that name so much better. I'm Cliff Masters. You're here about the room?"

"Yes, I am. Is it still available?"

He gave me an odd look. "Of course it is. Shall I show it to you?"

I wasn't sure what to make of this guy. "Sure, thanks."

"Come this way."

I followed him, admiring the knotty pine walls, the creaky wooden floors, and the gleaming cabinets full of beautifully colored glass figurines and vases. Somebody's interesting landscape art filled the walls. I thought briefly of the unusual murals on Winter's ceilings as I followed Cliff outside.

"This is it." He pointed to a strange-looking tent pitched near a long, odd-shaped pool. It was massive but wasn't quite oval or rectangular. I gaped at the tent. Cliff laughed, slapping his thighs. "You should see your face!"

"That's the room?" I asked, wondering why he thought it was so funny.

"Of course not. Only kidding. That's a sweat lodge. We

have sessions there once a week."

I nodded, though I had no idea what he was talking about.

"You ever been on a vision quest?" he asked.

"Nope. Never."

"Good. You'll come tomorrow night. You'll love it. Let me show you your room." We turned a corner, and he opened another door, and we walked inside. The room was tiny, but it was all I needed. There was a bed that looked fine to me, a hat rack for clothing, an armchair, and a card table. It was perfect.

"This room's been good luck for a lot of guys. You like it?"

"Very much."

"Cool. Let me show you the bathroom. There are sheets on the bed, and I'll give you a towel, but you'll be responsible for washing everything. Rent's due on the first of each month, but since you're here halfway through, I'll take twenty now, and you can pay forty on the first. Deal?"

"Forty a month sounds good, but you don't know anything about me though," I said.

He tilted his head to one side. "I think I do. You're a musician. You just arrived in town, you've got cool friends

"I opened my mouth, but he cut me off. "You were in a car with David Crosby, and I know Winter." He grinned. "And you need a place to stay. Am I close?"

I laughed. "Yeah. Pretty much. It's a deal." I put my duffle bag, and guitar on the bed then took out my wallet and gave him the twenty. I couldn't believe my good fortune. "Why's it so cheap?"

"You can pay me more if you like."

I laughed again. "No, no. I'm good with forty."

"Twenty, remember?" He waved the note at me.

"Right."

"Come on. I'll show you around."

The house was huge, and there seemed to be four

bedrooms and three bathrooms. He mentioned tunnels underneath the house that he'd show me another time.

"The hills behind this house have some really cool little man-made caves. They're pretty far out. I'll take you up sometime."

"Thanks." I'd never heard about these caves, but I was fascinated.

"Help yourself to anything in the fridge. Remember that in case you bring home something you really want. If you leave it in there, it's guaranteed to be eaten by somebody else. I gotta go now, but I'll see you later."

"Do I need a key?"

He looked at me as if I were crazy. "No key. No locks here."

"Oh. Okay." That surprised me, considering some of the beautiful stuff they had in the house, including shelves filled with some of the most fascinating books I'd ever seen. Winter had mentioned one of the men living in the house was a writer. Turned out it was Cliff. His room was filled with a collection of antique typewriters, and a canoe propped against the wall.

"There are two other guys here, both actors. Both nice. One of them talks to himself, but he's harmless. See ya!" He gave me a towel from the linen closet in the hallway and left the house. I lost no time in taking a shower. It was the first one I'd taken in two days. Back in my room, I put on fresh underpants, socks, and T-shirt, but kept the same jeans. I laced up a different pair of sneakers on my feet. I already felt better.

A part of me wanted to explore the house and maybe find those tunnels, but I really dug the idea of exploring the neighborhood. Besides, I now had to find a job and realized the uneasiness I felt was worrying about my parents.

The only thing I took with me was my guitar. I would die without it. It had been a wrench leaving the first one I'd ever owned, but just like my dog, I vowed to go home and get it one day.

Outside on the canyon, the air was crisp and cool. I glanced up the steep incline to the deep heart of Lookout Mountain and decided I could come back later and check it out. Just as I was heading back down Laurel Canyon, a couple came down the street chatting animatedly. My eyes almost fell out of my head. It was John Phillips, and his gorgeous wife, Michelle Phillips, of The Mamas and the Papas. She gave me a radiant smile. He tipped an imaginary hat to me.

"Good morning." She was as beautiful as she looked in photos and on TV.

I beamed at them, dying to say, "I love your music," but I was trying to be cool. I lived on the same street as The Mamas and the Papas!

"Good morning," I said back. I felt all warm and toasty inside as I fell into step with them walking down to the Canyon Country Store.

"Were you there last night?" John asked me.

"I was."

"What was it like?" Michelle asked, threading her arm through mine. She smelled like flowers after a gentle rain. I wanted to nuzzle her long, blonde hair, even though I was gay. "John drove down real early this morning and said the street was like a ghost town."

"It was intense, but nothing like the radio reports make it sound."

She nodded. "That's what David Crosby said."

Man, that guy got around!

We walked, the trip all too short for my liking, all the way to the steps of the store.

"I'm Michelle, and this is John." My favorite music goddess was as humble as she was beautiful.

"I'm Taris. Taris West."

"Have a beautiful day, Taris West." She smiled again, and

I wished I could have loved women. If I had grooved to them, I would be besotted with her and half-crazy with love by now. I almost stumbled along the road to the phone booth I'd seen outside the store. I slipped inside, deposited a dime, and called my parents. The operator informed me I'd need another dime. In spite of the morning chill, I was sweating. The telephone receiver felt greasy in my hand.

My mom answered on the third ring. "Hello?"

"Hi, Mom. It's me."

Silence. Then, "Taris?" She sounded as cold as the canyon air.

I wanted to say, "Of course it's Taris. Who else would I be?" Instead, I said, "Mom, I'm sorry. I shouldn't have left like that."

"No, you shouldn't have. And roping your brother and cousin into a race riot on the street!"

"It wasn't like that!"

"You were almost arrested!"

"No, I wasn't. We were just there. We were never at risk. Mom—"

"Your father is so upset I'm surprised he hasn't had a heart attack. Do you never think of anyone but yourself?"

"I—"

"And your cousin's girlfriend is pregnant!"

"That had nothing to do with me. I knew nothing about it until last night, and he only found out yesterday!"

"I know it had nothing to do with you." Her words came out like little chips of ice. "Ray told us everything. About how you're a homo."

This couldn't be happening. My mouth dropped open. I blinked, trying to breathe, trying to think.

"He said you and Justin used to fool around. My God! It's sick! You're *disgusting*. You know what this could do to his parents if they find out you're sexual deviants? If they ever find his body, he might not get a Catholic burial!"

I knew my mom would take it hard, but this was shocking. "Mom—"

"Don't call me that!" she shrieked. "Don't call me again! I can't live with this shame. I don't know whether to boil your bed sheets or burn them. You disgust me!"

She hung up on me. I stood for a long time holding the receiver, hoping I was imagining things and that she still loved me. I tried to picture her boiling my sheets, and my heart broke. I remained where I was until somebody tapped the window. I looked up to find that freak, Brent, shaking his head at me.

I hung up the receiver and opened the door, apologizing.

"Some of us have to get to work," he griped. He must have seen the look on my face because suddenly he squinted. "Everything okay?"

"Yes, fine," I lied, then walked down the hill toward Sunset on shaky legs. I kept replaying the conversation in my mind. It hurt me tremendously that Ray had violated my trust. It was my secret to share with my parents. Not his. I kept thinking about the radio announcer talking about the protests. Apparently, everything was being protested except gay rights.

I'd had hopes that the riot at Compton's Cafeteria in San Francisco in August might have ignited some change. I'd followed the radio reports with avid interest. Oddly, the newspapers up in Northern California had not covered it. It all started when the owner of the cafeteria began calling the police to report customers he didn't want in his establishment. They were transgender and transsexual individuals, and when the police began arresting them, tension mounted.

It all culminated one fateful night when the police, who were known to be particularly aggressive toward transgender women, attempted to arrest one, simply because she tried to buy a cup of coffee.

Things escalated fast. From what I heard, dishes and furniture were thrown, and the restaurant's plate-glass windows were smashed. A police car had all its windows broken out, and a newsstand was burned down. Many of the people involved were members of a group called the Vanguard. The reports said it was the country's first-ever gay youth organization.

My hopes had been dashed because the reports of that incident were like the ones from last night. I had a feeling people like me would be waiting a long time for justice, for equality. If we ever got it at all. It would take a different riot, a different time, for us to gain tolerance or even acceptance.

But we had started the fire. The youth the establishment had so condemned had ignited a torch that would burn brightly. We had started something. We would not be ignored. I wanted to weep but fought it. Rage swirled within me at my brother's treachery. I didn't blame him. Not really. I knew my brother better than anyone. He'd turned on me to save himself from months of acrimony. My mom had always been domineering. She always worried about what 'society' and the neighbors would think.

I let out a sigh. I was free. I was where I wanted to be. How funny, though. My college philosophy classes came back to remind me of Jean-Jacques Rousseau's words: "Man is free but is everywhere in chains."

Down on Sunset, I saw the mechanic from yesterday sweeping up debris from the riot. The gas station was a mess. I would have offered to help, but he saw me and instantly said, "I'm sorry your car got banged up pretty bad."

I followed him to it, stunned to see all the windows had been smashed. Somebody had slashed the tires, punched out the headlights, and the steering wheel was missing.

"Oh, man," I said. I hadn't expected this.

"I can try and find you another steering wheel, but it's

gonna be a big job fixing everything."

"Right," I said.

"I'm sorry," he said again.

"Not your fault." I took a deep breath. "I suppose we'll have to junk it." I'd write and tell Ray what happened. I knew he'd be upset, but then again, he'd given the car to me, so maybe he didn't care anymore.

"I'll give you five hundred dollars for it," the mechanic said. "Put it toward something new."

That surprised me. "Sure." I could tell he felt bad, but the money would help me in my new life. I didn't really need a car. Yet.

He opened his little mechanic shop and sat down in a grubby corner filled with strange bits of blackened car parts, shoved these aside, then pulled out his checkbook.

"What's your name again, son?"

"Taris West."

"Right. Your brother told me that." He wrote in neat little block letters, then tore off the check. It was on a Bank of America account. I banked with them, too, only I currently had a whopping three dollars and twenty-nine cents in mine.

"Thank you," I said.

"You need anything from inside it?"

I had all I needed, including some fine and not so fine memories. "No, thank you," I said and walked away from it.

All of it.

CHAPTER FIVE

Sunset was very quiet, just as Michelle Phillips had said. Nobody was around at Pandora's Box. I wondered if it was now going to be shut down. Clearly, the demonstration had changed nothing. The street felt dispirited. I checked my watch. Eight o'clock. Still early. I made a right and sauntered past the mostly shuttered stores. On my own now and with plenty of time, I had the chance to examine the clubs and shops I'd only heard about or seen photos of in newspapers and magazines. I was particularly enthralled by a club called The Sea Witch. It was designed to look like the rusted hull of a ship, complete with a nude mannequin with her arms raised as though trying to swim away from the wreckage out front.

A big sign announced, *Live Music Every Nite! Dance! Twist! Jerk! Now Appearing: Brain Train.*

I hadn't noticed that yesterday. I was excited to come and see them play. On my right stood Largo, a strip club, right next to a restaurant called Villa Nova. Beside that was Bank of America. I made a mental note to come and deposit my check when it was open.

There were so many music clubs I was in Heaven. Dean Martin's restaurant Dino's Lodge, The Roxy, The Trip, Sneaky Pete's, London Fog (which boasted a sign saying The Doors would be playing here) and the Galaxy next door also looked cool.

Across the road, I noticed a bakery called Pupi's. The enticing aroma of warm bread pulled me as if by a magical string and I dodged traffic getting over there. The sidewalk café had plenty of customers, and it looked as if this section of the Sunset Strip was a lot more... elegant than my section several blocks east.

I went inside and salivated over the delicacies in the pastry case. I ordered a cappuccino and, although I wasn't a cake guy, I had a feeling I could become highly addicted to their chocolate rum cake. I ate two slices and downed a second coffee before I felt like my old self again.

I sat at an outdoor table, wishing I'd thought to bring my notebook. I bristled thinking about how my brother claimed he'd written all the band's songs. We'd written them together, but since I had written lyrics and he'd been the music man, maybe he didn't think words counted. Somebody had left their *Los Angeles Times* newspaper on a chair, and I grabbed it. I was pleased to see the riot report was fairly accurate and that, for a change, a newspaper bothered to get their facts straight.

In the second paragraph, the report mentioned the marines who'd started throwing the first punches.

"Good afternoon," a voice said beside me. I glanced over. A handsome, older gentleman smiled at me. I checked my watch. Man, it was noon. I'd been here for hours.

"Good afternoon," I responded.

He smiled at me. "You seem surprised."

"I've been here for almost four hours."

He gave a small chuckle. "Actors have been known to linger here for hours. Enjoy." He stood, gave me a stiff little bow, and walked away. He'd been charming, but something about him made me think he'd known the darkness. I had a feeling he was an actor, but I couldn't place him.

A bunch of guys had been hogging a table all morning. I recognized Jack Nicholson and wondered who the others were. A tall, statuesque woman with a grumpy look on her face came out to me.

"You still here?" she asked, but I didn't think she meant to be unkind.

"May I ask you... The gentleman I was just talking to —"

"Yes, Mr. Novarro."

His name meant nothing to me.

"Ramon Novarro," she said louder, as though I were deaf.

"Thank you. I couldn't quite place him."

"It's been some time since he was in a movie, though I'm told he still sings. Can I get you a sandwich? Our roast beef is to die for."

"I would like that, thank you."

She returned with it a few minutes later. It looked delicious. Warm, plump with meat, and I forced myself not to drool. "You can pay when you're done." She hesitated. "You're not looking for work, are you?"

"Yes, as a matter of fact."

"I can give you work two days a week. All I have right now."

"Sounds good to me."

"Wonderful. Lunch is on me. Be here first thing in the morning. Six a.m. I need help with the baking."

Six a.m.? What was I doing? How could I be here at the crack of dawn when I would be listening to music all night? And besides, Winter had practically told me I could have a job at The Troubadour. I finished my sandwich quickly and headed back along Sunset. I went home, ignored the sweat seeping through my pores, and returned to the bank with my savings account booklet, depositing my check into it.

The teller looked at me as though she didn't trust me but accepted the deposit. I told her I had a new address, but she lifted a brow when I told her I didn't know the street number. "I just moved in here today," I said, embarrassed. "I'll come back with the actual street address."

"Do that."

"It's the old Tom Mix house." I had no idea why I told her that.

"I know that place. It's two-four-zero-one Laurel Canyon." She wrote down the address on a piece of paper.

"You know it?"

She pulled a face. "My brother was renting a room there until a few days ago."

My stomach dropped. "He was?" I swallowed. "What made him move?"

She winced. "Did you move into the small room by the pool?"

"Yeah! What gives?"

She bit her lip. "He says it's haunted and nobody lasts more than a week there."

Oh, great! "Okay," I said.

"Sorry. People are waiting. I'll update your file." She shrugged apologetically. I shuffled back up Sunset to the Canyon Country Store. Winter was already there when I arrived. He didn't seem mad that I was early. In fact, he seemed *damned* happy. He beckoned me to follow him, and we raced to his house on Kirkwood. He dragged me into his bedroom. I gazed up at the ceiling. More work had been done on the mural. Maybe this place was haunted, too.

He kissed me hard. Short, sharp kisses, then he took my face in his hands. "I want that ass," he snarled. I let him push me to the bed. He stripped my jeans and underpants down, and my cock sprang out at him. He let out a *tsking* sound as he had to stop and kick off my shoes and socks. I protested when one of my socks sailed out of the open window.

"Oh, look," he crooned softly. "Toys." His gaze swept over my cock and balls. He tongued me, my body on fire when he shouldered my legs apart and dipped his face between my thighs. He lapped at my asshole. I almost burst into tears. It was the first time he'd done this, and the feeling of a man's tongue on my ass was indescribable.

"You are gonna get fucked, and you will never forget it.' He squinted at me. "You been fucked before?"

"Yes." Silence fell between us. "Twice."

"Twice?" He gaped at me. "That's it?"

I nodded. "My boyfriend was, you know..."

"An idiot?"

"Closeted," I corrected. "Don't say mean things about him. He's dead."

"I won't say mean things since I plan to make you forget all about him."

That cracked me up. Six months ago, I thought I would die without Justin in my life. Now I was laughing at the thought of Winter trying to win me over.

He slipped my T-shirt up over my shoulders, quickly running his tongue against my nipples. He eased the T-shirt over my head and our eyes connected. He got undressed and moved back to the bed. He thrust his hips toward me, but I knew it was involuntary. We were so into each other, our cocks gravitated toward one another. I averted my gaze. I had to make him wait.

We were breathing hard. I pushed him back, and finally claimed his big juicy cock with my tongue. I sucked him for a bit. Justin always said I sucked like a whore. Damn it. I needed to stop thinking about him. I reached up to kiss Winter. His eyes were languid with desire. He upended me, and we seemed to fall into each other. Our cooks found their way into one another's mouths.

I needed to kiss him again. I pulled myself away from his cock and up to his face. I moved my mouth over his face and throat and down to his nipples. I loved how he squirmed every place I licked him, loved the salty taste to his skin. He was so hard now. I couldn't believe I could get him that hard just by kissing him.

It was my turn to taste him. One look from me, and he seemed to know what to do. His knees came up, and I kissed my way down his legs. They opened up to me, and I plunged my face to his ass. He bucked at the new contact with my tongue. I laved at his asshole, which was hot and wet.

"Stroke your cock for me," I commanded. He was jerking underneath me as my tongue entered him, then flicked up to his balls. His mouth dropped open, and he looked down at me with a burnished gaze. I took pity on him and started licking his ass again, using my thumb to rub circles on his ass.

"Oh... no... lick me... I'll do that."

I took my mouth off him, releasing the now-purple head with a pop. I slapped his ass lightly and sucked him into my mouth again, making him cry out. His hand moved slowly up and down his cock. He came hard and fast, his orgasm making me go off like a rocket.

After a pause, we got fired up again. My whole body reacted to his merest touch. I wanted him badly now. Justin had never taken his time with me because we simply didn't have it. I loved being in bed with this gorgeous man with the sound of The Supremes on somebody's radio drifting into the bedroom and the smell of sex on the air. He reached into his bedside drawer and produced a container of Vaseline. It turned me on for some reason. Justin had used olive oil.

"It goes back to three hundred and fifty B.C. as a personal lubricant," he'd said. At the time, it was all we had handy since we were in my parents' basement, and my dad used oil on his barbecue. I'd never been able to look at a roasted piece of meat the same way since.

My cock was bone hard when Winter lubed me up. He was ready for me but took his time entering me. It didn't hurt like it had with Justin. Everything was different with Winter, who seemed more sensual than—

I made a decision then and there not to think about Justin

again when I was in bed with Winter.

He fucked me deeply, and so slowly I thought I would go mad, but the orgasm I had was so peaceful and yet intense, I couldn't speak or think. He exploded outside of me in mid-thrust, then quickly shoved himself back into me. I wrapped my legs around him, and we rocked each other long after our bodies had stopped quaking.

We were both drenched as he rolled over and pulled me into his arms. He spooned me, and I closed my eyes. All I could see was him, laughing, playing the radio for me, singing songs. And I smiled. Even though I was sleeping.

We got out of bed around four o'clock, and he said, "Let's go for a walk." We showered and changed back into our clothes. He lent me a pair of his socks since one of mine had taken a vacation. He saw me pick up my guitar and said, "Will you leave that damned thing here?"

I shook my head. "No. My record got stolen last night, and I'm not taking any chances." I almost keeled over when the pocket of my guitar case crackled. The record was back. "It wasn't there this morning." I checked the interior of the case. *Pet Sounds* was still there.

His eyes gleamed at me. "And it got back in there while we were in bed?"

"Yes."

"I knew it. I heard somebody in here. Did you notice that damned mural?" He pointed to the ceiling. "It keeps being added to."

"I did notice that. But I didn't hear anyone in here just now."

"I'm not surprised, beautiful boy. You were snoring in my arms like a cute little bulldog."

"Hey!"

"It's true." He threw up his hands. "Let's take a walk, then

go grab a burger. I'll introduce you to the cats at The Troubadour, see if we can't get you a job."

"Well, I sort of already have one."

"You do?" He seemed stunned. "Where?"

"Pupi's."

"The actor's hangout? Food's great but the owner, man,
she's kinda freaky."

"Is she the grumpy dark-haired lady?"

"Marge. That's her. Well, at least you'll have access to some
good eats."

We walked outside, turned right heading away from Laurel Canyon and up toward Lookout Mountain. As much as he
wanted me to, I refused to leave my guitar. That and my
clothes were all I had.

"Do you think Brent's the one coming into the room and
painting and stuff?" I asked him.

"Naw."

"So who do you think it is?"

He shrugged.

"You don't think it's a ghost, do you?"

He looked at me. "The possibility has occurred to me."

"Nah. Can't be."

"It can't be Brent. He doesn't have the imagination to do
it," Winter said. He scratched his head. "You know, I've had
stuff taken in the house, but it always comes back."

"If you say so. I'm still not leaving my guitar there."

"Then don't." He grabbed me around the neck and kissed
my forehead.

I loved our walk, both for his tenderness and the view. It
was a beautiful canyon with gorgeous views of Hollywood in
front of us, Beverly Hills to the right, and, Winter pointed out,
far in the distance it was easy to spot the airport and, beyond
it, the ocean. I could even see airplanes landing on the run-
way.

He pointed out many homes with history attached to them and even took me into one of the caves Cliff had mentioned to me. It was a little eerie being in there because it was evident somebody was living there. Blankets, food, and a radio were stacked against the wall. We sat inside for a bit, and Winter turned on the radio. It crackled a little, but we laughed when *Winchester Cathedral* came on.

"I bet *Good Vibrations* is next," I joked. And I was right.

We replaced the radio and left the cave, heading back to Winter's house. I was surprised when he gestured to a Mustang parked near it. "These are my wheels," he said. It was quite nice to be driven in a car that was functional. I gazed out the window at the passing scenery.

"Tomorrow's my day off," he said. "I'll take you on a personal tour."

"I'd love that."

He reached across the street and squeezed my knee before returning his hand to the wheel.

"You know much about The Troubadour?" he asked me.

"Nope. Only that anybody who's anybody plays there."

"True." He grinned. "Lenny Bruce played there a few years ago. Did you hear about that show?"

I shook my head.

"Well, I wasn't there, of course, but he swore on stage. He said the word schmuck... and the next thing everybody knew, the police were there. They handcuffed him on stage."

"Schmuck is a swear word?"

"It was in nineteen-sixty-one."

"Wow."

We got to the club on Santa Monica Boulevard a little after six. Winter introduced me to the club owner, Doug Weston. He was super nice but told me he had a long waiting list for jobs.

"Don't worry," he said. "It moves fast. I'll put you on it

right now."

"Thank you," I said. I was astonished when he produced a massive wad of papers and added my name to it. I made a mental note not to hold my breath.

The evening was a wonderful one. I had no idea Buffalo Springfield had made their debut there earlier in the year, and they came to the stage for a couple of songs.

Neil Young and Stephen Stills were such guitar virtuosos I couldn't keep my gaze from their fingers.

I had one beer the whole night but felt high at the end of Winter's shift just from the sheer excitement of the place. I asked a lot of people if The Doors were in town and if they'd made it to the Whisky a Go-Go when hell broke loose on Sunset, but nobody seemed to know. I was dying to see them play live. I couldn't wait.

When we went home, Winter confessed that he hated going home. "My roommate is a nut. I can't throw him out because he paid a month's rent already, but he's weird. You know what I mean?"

"Yeah, I do."

That didn't stop us from going back there. I took Pet Sounds out of my guitar case, and we studied the cover. It was cool and peculiar at the same time. The Beach Boys and a bunch of goats. Seven of them, to be precise. They were feeding them pieces of apple, and I kept staring at the photo as we mowed through several cups of coffee and several playing of the record. *God Only Knows* struck me as the most beautiful song I'd ever heard. That's what love was, to my way of thinking. Loving and needing someone so much, the thought of life without them incites endless gratitude for that person.

We played it over and over.

"Man," Winter said. "He just gets it."

The more we played the album, the more we understood its incredible harmonies, unusual sounds, and intricate melodies.

"That sound there," Winter said at one point, "is supposed to be Brian Wilson crush Coca Cola Cans."

Later, we sloped off to bed. Brent hadn't showed up all night, and at first, we thought we'd lucked out. But after we drifted to sleep, Winter woke me up with kisses.

"I need you," he whispered. His gaze and his touch were so tender yet so passionate I was hard in an instant.

Winter moved over me, and our mouths met in a frenzy of kissing as he entered me easily. I was already warm and slick from the last time he'd taken me.

Suddenly, we heard Brent coming home.

"Fuck," Winter muttered into my ear right in the middle of the most righteous fucking. My legs were over his shoulders, and I hoped like heck that Brent didn't choose that moment to come into the room.

He didn't.

After a beat, Winter resumed fucking me like crazy. We almost laughed a few minutes later when the next sound we heard was *scrape, scrape. Stomp, stomp.*

I didn't get much sleep but was up early. I showered and changed back into my jeans, borrowed socks, and a clean T-shirt that belonged to Winter. I kinda liked wearing his stuff. It made me feel sexy.

"Leave the guitar here," he grumbled.

"No can do," I said.

He rolled his eyes. "Come on, I'll drive you down the hill."

I was touched. As we made the journey down in the dark, a couple of night creatures darted across the canyon in front of us.

"We're in the country, baby," Winter said, with a laugh. "Say, what time do you get off later?"

"No idea."

When we stopped outside Pupi's, Marge was inside, face pressed to the window, her eyes little black, burning coals.

"Aw, shoot. She's scary," Winter said. "I'm afraid to leave you here with her."

"I'll be okay," I said, sounding more confident to my own ears than I really felt.

"Well, I'll swing by later for coffee. Pretend I've kissed you."

"I feel it," I said, grinning at him. I was starting to seriously be crazy about this guy. My good mood lasted me through a rough shift where I burned myself twice on the oven, and three times counted out wrong change.

We worked like mad for four hours. I got a brief break from the hot ovens at ten when I switched to working the bakery counter. At noon, I got a fifteen-minute coffee break and wandered across the road to check out Holly's Harp, a store filled with dresses made out of Spanish shawls. She also sold fringed vests and tie-dyed shirts. With my first paycheck, I decided I'd buy one of those shirts. My mother would freak if she saw me in it, which made me even more determined to buy one.

Back at the café, I was thrilled when Winter showed up around one but stifled a groan when I saw him accompanied by Brent.

Oddly, a few of the actors' tables around us suddenly emptied. Marge wasn't happy.

"They bug me," she told me inside the café. "All those *thespians*." She made it sound like a dirty word. "But they make my place look successful. I don't like when they go."

She banged the cash register shut. I had no idea what she was talking about. She was always screaming at them to go get a job and to quit taking up space at the sidewalk tables. Jack Nicholson and actor Warren Oates hung out all day playing chess and just laughed at her, but I was frankly embarrassed by her outbursts.

After about an hour, Winter left. "What time do you finish?" he asked. Marge overheard us and said, "Four o'clock, but if you do some actual work soon, you can finish now."

Winter raised his brow at me. "I'll pick you up," he said and left, Brent following him. I was certain I spotted blue paint on Brent's jeans, but maybe I was wrong.

I wiped down a couple of tables, counting the minutes until four. The actor Ramon Novarro caught my eye.

"She's not blaming you, is she?"

I straightened. Every muscle in my body ached.

"No. Why would she do that?"

"Because of, you know..."

"What?" I asked. What the heck was going on?

"Your friend," he whispered, his frightened gaze casting around the place.

"My friend?"

"Yes." He gave me a significant look I couldn't read.

"You know about him, of course." He gave me a quizzical look.

"No. I don't." What the hell was he trying so hard not to tell me?

"Well, not everybody knows, but some people do, and they are afraid."

"What of?"

He looked at me strangely. "You really don't know, do you?" He shook his head and bit his lip. He leaned closer and said, "Your friend is CIA."

CHAPTER SIX

CIA? Was he kidding?

For the rest of my shift, I pondered never seeing Winter again, but he had custody of my guitar. When he showed up at four, he could see I was tense.

"What's wrong?" he asked. "Apart from your gorgeous boss?"

"Is it true you're CIA?" I blurted.

He shook his head. "Man. Word really got around, didn't it?"

I stared at him. "You mean it's true?"

"Of course, it isn't true. I'm not CIA." He paused. "Brent is."

"Brent?" I almost screamed. Suddenly it all made sense. He was too wacky to be real.

Winter drove us away, and we headed back up the canyon. "I can't say much, but well, he came to the house via my cousin, Spencer, who called me from San Francisco and insisted Brent stay at the house. After a day, I called Spencer, and told him I couldn't handle the guy."

He paused when we reached a red light at Doheny. "That's when Tony Spencer me that Brent was CIA. Or rather, he said ex-CIA, that he'd dropped out and was trying to start a new life." He turned and looked at me. "Don't stare at me like that. I have no idea if he's ex-CIA or current. But he's paid his rent, and he's a damned nuisance." He gripped the wheel, a muscle working in his cheek. "He knows I'm gay and doesn't care. He says he's unsure of his sexuality, but that he might be gay, too. I made it clear that he ain't experimentin' with me."

"Good," I said.

"Everybody's running from something, Taris. He's no different, but it worries me that some people know about him."

"Me, too."

We got to Laurel Canyon, and he waited to make a left turn.

"What do you *really* think he wants here?" I asked.

Winter shrugged. His face took on a closed look. "I don't know. I have some theories, but I hope I'm wrong."

"You can trust me. Tell me what you think."

He glanced at me, amusement in his gaze. "This from the man who's petrified to leave his guitar with me."

"You're right," I said. "I'm an asshole."

We both laughed, and a vehicle behind us honked. Winter made the turn, and he said, "We'll talk about this later. I don't like to gossip, and I have nothing definitive to say anyway."

"Fair enough." I didn't want to be like my mom, who couldn't let a topic slide. And, oh, boy, I sure didn't want to appear moody or quarrelsome.

"Can we stop at my place?" I asked. "I need to get some clean clothes."

"Sure," he said. "I want to check it out anyway."

We walked inside the house to some weird music pouring out of it. In the living room, Frank Zappa was jamming with some people I didn't know. Cliff was perched in the corner and waved. It was hard to mistake him with his unusual hair and mustache.

"Everybody, this is Taris. Taris East."

"West," I corrected. "Hi, everybody." Frank Zappa grinned at me. "Hey, Winter. How ya doin'?"

"Great, thanks. And you?"

"Freaky, man."

He was a character. He stood at one point, and I couldn't

help staring at the crotch of his pants. They were so tight I could see everything. Clearly, he was wearing no underpants, and he was *massive. I bet Mrs. Zappa is one happy woman.*

Once again, Winter seemed to know everybody. Frank waved a hand around the place. "The guys are trying to convince me to take over the lease on this place. I'm thinking about it."

We blew past them all. Cliff stopped me. "You're coming by tonight, I hope. It's the vision quest."

"Oh, sure," I said. "I'll try."

"Can I come, too?" Winter asked, sounding excited.

"Of course, baby." Cliff went back to reading his book.

"What time?" I asked.

"Sunset," Winter and Cliff said in unison.

In my room, Winter grabbed me and kissed me. "Those vision quests are freaky, man. You wait. You'll write songs you never knew you had in you, afterward. I think we should bring Brent, too."

"Do we have to?"

He grinned. "I have a sneaky plan. "He's been obsessed with this place. I bet he wants to move in." His words came out in a rush. "Somehow, the last tenant left, and you got in before he even knew it. He says he's fascinated by the history of the place. I think he wants to watch one of the residents." He held up a hand. "Just my theory, though. I bet he'd trade with you. You could have his room, though we'll be bunking of course."

"Brilliant!" I said.

His eyes took on a dreamy glow. "Just think, no more scraping and bumping."

Yeah. I could imagine it just fine.

We hung out at the house, though I did worry about my guitar being back at Winter's. He said I needed to quit fretting about *stuff* and trust the universe.

"Trust me," he said, and I did.

A bunch of guys and gals turned up around sunset, everyone talking about going to Bido Lito's to listen to The Doors, who were supposed to be playing there. Cliff, who had spent all afternoon getting things ready in the backyard became upset.

"We're supposed to be having a vision quest!" he screamed.

"Freaky," Frank said.

Most of the people trooped into the backyard and, as some lit incense sticks and others played guitar, a Native American man stood next to the tent and intoned something that sounded like "Doo doo doo." I tried not to laugh. People seemed so serious. They swayed and nodded, holding their arms to the sky. I kept thinking about The Sea Witch. I could be there tonight, listening to music, instead of this nonsense.

The Native American man kept chanting. I looked around but couldn't see Frank Zappa. Maybe he'd left. I didn't recognize anyone but Cliff and Winter. Somebody passed around a joint.

"In nineteen-forty-eight, actor Robert Mitchum got arrested smoking marijuana right here at this house. He got a two-month jail sentence," Cliff told everyone. "Thank God some things do change."

Next thing I knew, we were all squeezing inside the tent. It was stifling hot. Everybody sat, the Native American man in the middle of the crowd. Cliff passed around a half shell of a coconut. The brown, swishy contents looked dubious, but Winter took a healthy slug, so I did too. I felt like I'd swallowed slime and tried not to gag. I experienced nothing at first except maybe feeling a little hotter than before. Suddenly, I couldn't stand to be in my own skin. Everything itched. I was on fire, and not in a good way. I stood, scratching at myself.

Winter grabbed me and hauled me down. "It's starting,"

he said. "The vision is coming." His eyes looked vacant and frightening. I wanted to throw up. And I wanted to fly. I was outside, inhaling great gulps of air. For some reason, Sylvia Plath's poem, Ariel, came to me. A haunting female voice recited lines from it.

Man, I finally get that poem! She wanted to fly, too!

I gasped when I saw Justin sitting outside the tent. He raised his hand in greeting. He wore his Air Force uniform, the last thing I'd seen him in. I started to cry. He said something, but his words were drowned out by stupid Brent, who sat beside him naked, beating his bongo drums.

"What is it?" I asked, my heart breaking. Justin looked so different. So sad and so old.

"There's nothing to say. You were the Indian summer of my heart. I'm sorry I chose to leave. I'm sorry for the knowledge that we will die apart."

"Freaky man," Brent said, and I screamed.

The next thing I knew I was running down the canyon. I wanted to get away. I needed to drive. To fly. To soar. I wanted skin like fur. Thoughts raced. Leaves rattled in the trees.

He's gone. He's gone. He's gone.

I knew for sure Justin was dead. It was okay. I'd known it. I needed to talk to someone who knew him. I ran and ran but got lost. The canyons swallowed me up. David Crosby drove past me in his Mustang, flashing me a peace sign. Three girls sitting in the vehicle with him sang *California Dreamin'*.

Brent followed, waving a paintbrush.

I ran down to the Canyon Country Store phone booth, determined to call Ray. I couldn't get near the phone, though. There were snakes all over it. I sat on the steps and looked up at the sky.

A car horn honked. I looked over, and it was Ramon Novarro. "Are you okay?" he asked.

"I'm afraid of snakes," I said.

He came over to me. "You're having a bad trip," he said. "Let me take you home." I got into his car, wondering where Winter was. I turned, and he was in the backseat, saying, "I never loved my commanding officer. I regret that I was ever with him. You do believe that, don't you?"

"Oh, yes, Lady Godiva," I said, hoping the snakes hadn't gotten into the car.

Ramon drove me to his house. It was a sprawling ranch style thing. Inside, he fluttered around like a man not used to having visitors. He played piano for me as I sat on the sofa, listening to his splendid voice. A snake slithered across the piano.

Oh, no. Time to leave.

"You must see the dildo Rudolph Valentino gave me," he said.

"Was it a snake?"

"One might call it that." He held up a lead dildo encrusted with gems.

"Have you called Lady Godiva?" I asked.

"No. She is running late."

Nothing made sense, yet it all seemed perfectly clear. I turned and watched as Winter told his parents he had to leave the Air Force.

"You're queer?" his father sneered. "Here's a dime." He flipped it at him. "Call somebody who cares."

"Hey!" I yelled. "Don't talk to him like that." I walked out of the house, Winter suddenly there holding my hand.

"It's okay," he said. "It will all stop now."

The next thing I knew, I was back in the tent with him, and he was holding me tight.

I was very disturbed by the vision and worried about the implications of it.

A lot of people were troubled. Some had experienced nothing at all. Outside the tent, I could breathe again. The Native American man and Winter sat beside me on the ground.

"What worries you the most about what you saw?" the man asked me.

"I'm worried that my friend Justin is alive. He looked old in my dream. Or vision. I'm worried he is being held captive somewhere in Vietnam. I can handle not seeing him again, but I couldn't handle thinking he is suffering."

"In Native American medicine, for that's what this is, seeing a young person as old means they have returned to the mother earth." The man patted the ground. "Your friend is gone. He is with the great guardian spirit, but he will always be with you. One day when you are in trouble, his soul will call to you. If you see his face, know you are in danger. But nothing can touch him now. Heed whatever warnings he sends you."

He turned to Winter. "Your experience was so much more joyous."

Winter nodded. "I'm at peace when I'm with Lady Godiva here."

The man smiled and left us alone.

"How did you know my vision?" I asked Winter.

"We're connected. How about the snakes and the dildo?" He shook his head. "As Frank would say, 'Freaky, man.'"

I was exhausted after the vision quest. I couldn't even absorb that I had a dream and that Winter had shared it. We went to my room. Brent was lying on my bed, his bongos beside him.

"Hey," he said, raising his head. He smelled of beer and seemed dead drunk. "Mind if I crash here?"

"No." This was weird.

"Pack your things," Winter said to me. "You're moving in with me."

"I'll come tomorrow to get my stuff," Brent mumbled and turned over on his side. He stuck his thumb in his mouth and sucked on it as he went right back to sleep.

We went home, marveling about the experience. Winter couldn't wait to try again. I wasn't so sure I could deal with it.

"That was too weird," I said.

"I understand, but it will make sense one day, and then you'll want to try again."

"Do you really regret your relationship with your commanding officer?" I asked.

"Hell, yeah. He didn't respect me." He shook his head. "I was young and impressionable."

"How old are you?"

"Twenty-eight. I feel a lot older sometimes." He paused. "Do you want to call your brother?"

"Isn't it kinda late?" I checked my watch. Only eight-thirty. Wow. That vision quest seemed to have gone on for days. "Yeah. I do."

"Don't be scared. I'm here."

"Okay, thanks."

"And if it's awful, you'll hang up, and I'll still be here."

"Cool." I felt safe doing it with Winter beside me. We walked down to the store. The phone booth was empty, and there were no snakes, thank God. I put in my money and called home. My brother answered.

"Ray," I said.

"Shit. Taris. Are you okay?"

"Yeah."

"I'm so sorry, man. I hate what Mom said to you. I think she regrets it, too. I catch her crying sometimes, but then she gets angry and calls you names. It's so weird you're calling tonight. I'm moving out."

"You are?" I couldn't help adding, "For real this time?"

"Yeah. I'm getting married." He didn't sound happy about it.

"Who to?"

"Jessamine. She's having my baby."

I couldn't believe what I was hearing. "I thought it was Will's baby."

"Yeah, well, her parents don't like me, so she pretended to be with him."

"They don't like you?" This was news to me. "And what about Will? How's he handling all of this?"

"Jessamine used to sneak out at night to meet me, remember?"

I recalled it now. My dad had thought it was harmless, but then Jessamine wasn't his daughter. I'd forgotten about all this because it had been a couple of years ago.

"So, what, she was seeing you, *and* Will?"

"Well, yeah. But they never had sex. Not real sex. They were naked a lot and fooled around. I think he was shocked when he found out she was pregnant, but she eventually told everyone the truth." He blew out a sigh. "Now Will hates me. Says I've ruined his life. He won't talk to me, and today. Oh, man. It was a nightmare, Taris. Jess and her parents came over, and Mom made those horrible stuffed celery things she loves and meatballs with grape jelly, and poor Jess threw up everywhere, all over Mom's shag pile carpet."

I couldn't help it. I had to laugh.

"And you know how much she *luves* that carpet. Jess is having bad morning sickness issues, although, with her, it's all-day sickness."

My God. And my parents think I have problems... I still couldn't get over what he'd done to Will, who'd been crazy over that girl.

"I'm sorry I never told you," he said. "But Jess knows you're... you know..."

"Gay?"

"Right, right. And she doesn't trust you. Listen, I'm moving in with her parents."

"Oh, that'll be fun." I blew out a sigh. Ray had gone home to a tighter noose than ever.

"Mom and Dad threw me out of the house. I have to get a job. Can you believe it?"

"Of course you do," I said. "I have a job."

"You do?" he seemed shocked. So was I. What the heck did he think was going to happen in L.A.? Boy, I hadn't thought about the consequences of running off with Ray and Will before.

"The only reason I picked up the phone is that I'm waiting for Jess to come get me. It hasn't been fun, Taris. And I really miss you. I wish I could talk to you."

"Me, too," I said.

"But I promised Jess I'd cut off all ties. I'm taking Brutus with me. He's my dog, too. And that way a part of you will be with me. Oh, God. They're home. Gotta go."

He hung up on me.

I dropped the receiver and went home with Winter. He didn't know what to say when I repeated the conversation to him.

"And I thought I got the booby prize with *my* family," he said.

We walked down to Sunset. Things were quieter tonight. The police motorcycles seemed to be driving in circles. Pandora's Box was closed. A few downhearted kids hung outside, but they were bang out of luck. No music. No teen stampede.

They followed us over to The 5th Estate, which was hopping. Winter and I ordered sandwiches and coffee. We both wanted more, but we were also anxious to get home. Halfway up the hill, a car stopped beside us. It was Ramon Novarro.

Wow. This was really spooky. He offered us a ride, and we took it. Winter sat in front with me. The ride was over fast. Mr. Novarro dropped us at the corner of Kirkwood and gave us an enigmatic smile.

"You are lucky to have each other," he said. "I, too, expect company tonight." He gave us a friendly wave and drove off.

Back at the house, we went into the backyard and took off our clothes. For some reason, we both wanted to be naked in the lush grass.

"There's a dead squirrel in the toilet," I said.

"How romantic."

I laughed. I couldn't believe I'd almost spoiled the mood. We lay beside one another, counting stars. We started to kiss, touching one another with reverent fingers. I wanted him to fuck me, but we had no lube.

"Stay there," my own personal, gorgeous wood nymph said and darted off into the house. He returned with the Vaseline and a couple of beers. The beer felt good after the peyote. My dry, scratchy throat felt better, and my cock had never been harder.

I wanted Winter badly, and he knew it. He took the beer from me and kissed me with chilly lips that tasted of love.

From somewhere, loud music was playing, and I loved it. All strings. Winter and I took turns sucking each other's cocks. He put me on all fours in the moonlight and licked me from behind. It felt so good. I braced myself for his cock, his body arching into mine. The small moment of discomfort gave way to searing pleasure. Winter held my hips and fucked me hard and fast. I lowered my body down and my ass higher, knowing it would give him even greater joy.

We came so fast, almost too fast, that it took our breaths away.

"Bed," he whispered, against my damp neck. He pulled out of me and took me inside.

That night we heard no bumping and scraping.

But in the morning, somebody had been at work adding new figures to the mermaid mural.

CHAPTER SEVEN

What happened on our little patch of Sunset never seemed to make much of a ripple on the rest of the street or anywhere else, for that matter. As days turned to weeks, there were a few more nighttime skirmishes on the Sunset Strip, but nothing like the first one.

On December 3, Winter and I were delighted when *Winchester Cathedral* became the number one single across the country, displacing *You Keep Me Hangin' On* by the Supremes. After a one-week run, it was knocked off by The Beach Boys' *Good Vibrations*, only to rebound to the top spot the following week.

Two weeks later it was kicked off the top for good by *I'm a Believer*, by a hot new band called The Monkees. They even got their own TV show.

On December 7th, the news hit the radio that Sonny and Cher had been dropped as the Grand Marshals for the Rose Parade due to take place on New Year's Day.

They had been axed by the organizers because of their support of the kids affected by the club curfews. The news shocked everyone, especially when I saw Sonny on Sunset the same day and he told me and Winter that he'd found out about it the same way as everybody else.

"I heard it on the radio," he said. "Can you believe it?" He said he and Cher were devastated, but that they stood behind their support of the teenagers who'd fought the curfew.

Each day I went to work, a different club had been closed, and literally shuttered. Wooden boards had been nailed over some doors and windows. The 'establishment' clearly wanted live music out of the Strip. It was a tragedy in the making. So far, twelve clubs had been eliminated. They wanted the music to die.

Things were freaky, man, on the Strip. My boss asked me to take a food delivery to a house on Woodrow Wilson Drive. I tried hard to imagine the former US president, for whom it had been named, living on the spidery street that jutted off Laurel Canyon. It was a brick, timber, and white-painted house with gabled arches and a giant weeping willow in the front yard that had been trimmed by a butcher of a tree trimmer. I wondered if Brent had been here.

I knocked on the door, and a man with a pillowcase on his head and nothing else on his body opened the door a crack and peered out at me.

"Oh. Food," he muttered and handed me a twenty-dollar bill. He shut the door in my face. This would be repeated for several days. I didn't mind the door slamming too much because half of it was a massive tip for me.

On December 9th, according to constant radio reports, FBI Special Agent Wesley G. Grapp had just nabbed a wanted man.

Donald C. Ward, the twenty-year-old manager of The Sea Witch, had been arrested by FBI agents on a federal warrant and was being held on $1500 bail. He was accused of failing to report for induction into the armed forces.

That got everybody buzzing. Some people talked about pitching in money for his bail; others said they wanted to stay away from it.

The Sea Witch staff seemed to think they could do fine without its manager.

"Business as usual," workers insisted to anyone who asked.

We all understood their need to carry on. The Doors were

back in town and had been booked at The Sea Witch. They were to be the resident house band for the next eight nights. Being one of the few clubs left on the Strip, everybody showed up in force. Their music was awesome, and I was impressed with lead singer Jim Morrison's stage presence. He commanded that stage. Everybody drank in his swagger, his singing, and the way he laughed at himself when he tripped and nearly fell.

The club emptied out a little after eleven o'clock. Winter urged me to hurry home with him. "Somebody just said the cops are on their way here."

We hightailed it up the canyon but never heard a siren or a single scream. We heard nothing, until the morning when somebody came over to the house and told us Brent was missing.

Within twenty-four hours, we learned Brent had chosen to disappear from the canyon and our lives.

My former roommates mentioned that he'd left behind what looked like a magician's kit. Oddly, they also discovered professional oil paints and a folding stepladder hidden in the cellar. Brent took off after Cliff was the one who introduced Brent to Donald C. Ward. He felt terrible about it. Then they had a fight when Cliff awoke in the middle of the night to find Brent painting on Cliff's bedroom ceiling.

Cliff and his roommates found several pieces of bark hidden in the cellar with drawings of mermaids and starfish, just like the images that had been painted in the Kirkwood house.

That explained a lot... A CIA agent who had been watching The Sea Witch and who crept around painting murals everywhere. His secret passion, we learned, was to paint.

"He's a closet artist," Winter said. "I don't get it. If you want to paint, paint."

"Yeah," Frank Zappa said when we all sat around talking about it one night. "Just let your freak flag fly, man."

* * * *

Our lives went on, Winter and I so happy and, unbelievably, we never had a single argument. His cousin came and went, and finally told us he had to give up the house because Janis Joplin was focusing on a new album up north.

"She wants me there all the time. She buys me gifts. And, she has the best shoes," he told us. She has a pair that have hourglasses for heels. I could really dig a pair of my own."

We all moved out, Winter and I going back to my room in the log cabin house.

Cliff was still there, and we had a lot of weird and wonderful people dropping in at all hours of the day and night. One night, I awakened in the middle of the night to see a naked man curled up in the corner. It was Jim Morrison. He was painting something. I could smell the linseed oil.

Winter shot up in bed, yelling, "What the hell are you doing here?"

"Chillin'," Jim Morrison said in a strange voice.

He slept until morning after that when he shook us awake and invited me and Winter over to his house to see his artwork. I'd had no idea he was a painter.

We threw on clothes while he walked around looking for his. He found jeans and a torn shirt.

"I think my woman and I may have had fight last night," he murmured, slipping on the ruined fabric. "Things get pretty intense between us."

Winter made coffee, and we ate the last of the instant oatmeal. Jim was anxious to get home.

"Pamela's gonna hate me," he kept saying.

We followed him down to Laurel Canyon. His house was on Rothdell Trail right behind the Country Store and had a hell of a lot of steps to get to it.

Like Woodrow Wilson, Rothdell and other streets were all considered The Canyon. When we finally glimpsed his pieces, I realized many of them were identical to the ones hanging in the log cabin house.

Jim nudged me. "You need a chair in your room, man." With a flourish, he pointed to one against the wall. "I made this for you."

I stared at it. The work was detailed and colorful, but um, it only had three legs.

"I'll give it to you for twenty dollars," he said.

"It's missing a leg," I said.

"All right, then. Ten. But it's not meant to be useful. It's art."

"Okay, I said and counted out ten singles. I thought it was kinda classy to buy art from a music legend with my coffee shop tips.

The next day, I was delivering food again to the house on Woodrow Wilson. I'd gotten used to the guy who didn't say much, so I was surprised when a woman came to the door. Even more surprised to see it was Mama Cass Elliott. Noise filtered out from inside.

"Come in," she said.

I walked in, the scent of patchouli oil strong on the air. A group of people was sitting around, music filtering from all the walls. I spotted Steven Stills and Graham Nash. I'd read somewhere he and Mama Cass were great friends. I wished I could have stayed and hung out, but I had to go back to work.

She wore a purple dress with shimmering blue sleeves and copious amounts of bracelets and rings. With a jolt, I realized she was pregnant.

"You look beautiful, um, Mama."

"Call me Cass," the woman with one of the greatest voices in rock and roll said to me.

She seemed slimmer in life than on stage or TV. "How long

you been in the canyon?"

"Ah, this is my second month."

She frowned. "You're a musician, right?"

"Right." I hadn't gotten around to writing more than a couple of songs, but I intended to do better. Between work, being with Winter and hanging out playing music with our friends, putting words on a page by myself didn't always have much appeal.

"You're working too hard," she said. "I know Belinda's is looking for a new sales associate and you won't be run off your feet waiting on tables all day."

"I can't work there," I said.

"Why not?"

"There's a sign in there saying, 'No Nellie Trading.' It's against everything I stand for."

"Are you gay?" she asked, her expression pained.

"Yes," I had to admit it.

"Well then, of course, you should fight against it." She raised a fist. "David!" she shrieked.

David Crosby appeared beside her in his usual swirl of reefer smoke.

"We need a ride down to Sunset. We're going to confront the owner of Belinda's."

I gulped. Was she serious?

Her word must have been law because David didn't question it. He gave me a wave and handed me his guitar to hold. We hurtled down the canyon in his Mustang. I got jostled around the backseat but held onto the guitar with both hands, hoping we didn't crash. The man seemed to know only three speeds. Slow, Fast, and Welcome to Emergency.

Cass sat up front, muttering, "Love is love." She was a fine woman, I decided. She jumped out of the vehicle as we pulled up outside the store.

"Are you coming, David?" Cass bawled.

"I'm double-parked," he said.

I handed him his instrument and climbed out of the car.

"She scares me," David said, but he had a smile on his face.

I followed her inside, where Cass stalked the cramped rows of bric-a-brac until she found the sign. She plucked it from its space on the wall and stalked to the counter where two women stared at her.

"Listen here," Cass said, thrusting the hateful sign in their faces. "This sign is offensive. Do you hear me? Who are *you* to tell other people who they can and cannot love? Now, my friend here is a Nellie Boy. And if he wants to kiss a man here, or trade comic books with him, he can. Okay? Do you understand?"

The women nodded.

"If *anyone* wants to kiss here, they can. Get it? Got it?"

The woman nodded.

"Good." Cass whirled on her heel, beckoning me. I followed. She ripped up the sign, leaving a trail of paper behind us. Outside, David was waiting for us, the engine still running.

"I have to go to work," I said. She'd done something nice for all gay men, so I hated to ask her for money, but I still needed to bring my boss cash for the food.

"Did I pay you?" Cass asked as she got into the passenger seat.

"No. And I hate to ask but—

"David! Give the man some money."

David juggled his guitar in one hand and pulled a couple of bills from his pocket. He handed me two crumpled bills. "Keep it," he said.

Cass banged the car door shut and one of her own songs, *California Dreamin'* came on the radio. She laughed. "It never gets old hearing your music on the radio." She and David belted out the chorus as they drove away. I wished I could have gone with them. I glanced back at the store, determined to bring Winter in one day and kiss him full on the lips.

I told Winter the story when I got off my afternoon shift, and he grinned.

"You're *my* Nelly Boy," he said, strumming his guitar. "And I plan to kiss you inside that shop. And wherever else I feel like. A lot."

* * * *

December turned into a beautiful month for us. We read, wrote poetry, and decided to take a crack at writing music together.

"I've even thought of a name," Winter told me. "What do you think of The Nelly Boys?"

I opened my mouth, and he laughed. "Kidding! I do have a good one, though. Winter West. Or West Winter."

"Winter West," I said. I loved the sound of it. It would make people think. It might encourage other musicians to head west this winter. Or the next.

He took to calling me West unless we were in bed. Then I was Taris.

We took long walks, made love, worked, ate, and listened to music. I never tired of his company.

One morning, I woke him and started stroking him. His cock got hard for me instantly, fire dancing in his eyes. I'd never been the aggressor sexually, and he seemed to delight in the way I commanded his cock and his mouth. I slaved over his pleasing erection, sucking in his full length. He let out a strangled cry, and I released him, only to claim him with my lips once more.

He thrashed about on the bed, the way he always did when he wanted to be deep inside him. I mounted him, poising my ass over his cock head. He gripped my hips, his gaze searing into mine. He worked hard to get himself in me, but for me, it was ecstasy all the way. My cock grew harder, and he released his right hand to cuff my cock head. He managed to raise me up and lifted his head to suck me for a moment.

"If I wasn't a jealous guy," he huffed as I worked my ass over his cock, pulling him in inch by inch, "I'd love to watch another guy suck you while I'm fucking you."

The idea alone drove us into a frenzy. I ground down on his cock to the base. Riding him like this made it feel as though he was inside me deeper than ever. That and the imagery of having my cock sucked while we fucked made me come with a roar.

Winter wasn't far behind me. He came so hard it felt like a tidal wave in me. I wanted to feel like that every day.

We loitered in bed for another hour, our limbs wrapped around each other.

I had the day off, it being Christmas Eve, and we had three invitations. Two for Christmas Eve and one for Christmas Day. We'd decided we'd divide our time between our neighbors, and the Wilsons on Christmas Eve, and Cass Elliot's on Christmas Day. She wanted all her friends to come and meet her new friend, a singer-songwriter from back East called Joni Mitchell.

"You'll love her. I swear!" Cass insisted.

"I don't care where we go," Winter said, "as long as we're together."

I felt the same way. We went to our Christmas Eve dinners, which were uneventful until we stopped by the Canyon Country Store on our way home for a bottle of milk.

The owner told me he had a message for me. "Some guy called Ray keeps calling. I told him you don't live here."

"Sorry." I cringed. We went outside, and while Winter shot the breeze with some of our friends hanging out on the street, I called Ray at the number I was given.

"Hey," he said, sounding depressed. "Merry Christmas. You got my message."

"That's why I'm calling. Everything okay?"

"No. Not really."

"What's wrong?"

He was quiet so long I thought he might have walked away from the phone. "Jessamine is just like Mom." Before I could respond, he said, "She has old-fashioned ideas, and she's intolerant. I'm not letting her control me anymore." He drew a breath. "You're my brother, and I miss you. I want to see you, and I want you to be a part of our lives when our baby's born."

"I'd like that." I was so touched. This was the best Christmas gift he could have given me.

There's just one small problem."

"What's that?"

"She doesn't want the dog, and Mom and Dad don't want him. Can you come get him?"

"Of course I can," I said. *Man, the best double Christmas gift ever!*

"Can you come up and get him before New Year?"

I glanced at Winter. "One way or another, I will. Yes."

We ended our call, and I repeated everything to Winter. He grinned.

"I couldn't have planned this better," he said.

"Why's that?"

"Not telling you until tomorrow." He grinned at me.

We raced home to make hot chocolate, built a fire, and promised to stop each other from opening our gifts.

At four o'clock the next morning, we exchanged gifts. We'd bought each other the same tie-dyed shirt from Holly's Harp. We got a good laugh out of that one. Winter had a craving for hamburgers for breakfast, so we drove down to the musicians' hangout, Barney's Beanery. It was closed. We peered into the window, and I was shocked to see a sign affixed to the entryway just outside saying, Faggots Stay Out.

"We can't go anywhere," Winter said, sounding as hurt as I felt.

"We'll come back when they're open and tear it down," I promised.

He said nothing for a moment. Then, "I may never eat hamburgers again. I know where we can go. The only place in town not celebrating Christmas. Canter's Deli."

"Sounds good to me."

Other people seemed to have the idea. The place was packed, and I fell in love with it the second I saw it. We joined a line separated from the booths filling the gigantic café, separated by a red velvet rope. After a quick breakfast of omelets and coffee, we loaded up on pastries and whitefish salad at the service counter. We would have some for us, and some for our hostess that evening, Cass Elliot.

We returned to the house, and I wouldn't have been surprised to see Frank Zappa sitting there saying, "Freaky, man." Who I *did* see was John Phillips, who was hanging out with Cliff.

Winter and I actually got to jam with them. It was so much fun.

"We need to write some songs," Winter said to me. We went back to bed with our food stash and started to work out a song. We soon gave up. Sex and sleeping were much too alluring.

Neither Winter nor I talked to our families that day. He held me in his arms and said, "This is the first Christmas I haven't been miserable and lonely. Thank you for getting into my life."

I kissed him. "Thank you for being in mine. The only thing I miss is my dog."

"Well, I have some good news. The Doors are doing a private show New Year's Eve up in Santa Barbara. They invited us to be part of the crew."

"That's awesome! When did you speak to them?"

"They're here in town, and I spoke to Ray Manzarek, and he says they'll have a van, and in lieu of payment, we can go up and get Brutus on New Year's Day."

"When did you come up with this idea?" I asked, impressed.

"The minute I knew your brother didn't want your fantastic dog. We can stay with friends of Ray Manzarek's that night and come home January second. Then we have to hit the music hard."

I was ecstatic. I went down to the Canyon Country Store and called my brother Ray the news.

"Not until the first?" he whined. "Okay. She'll have my balls for this."

She already has them, I wanted to say but didn't.

We took our unopened boxes of pastries to Christmas dinner. Cass was sweet and appreciative, but when I looked around, realized she'd gone to a lot of trouble to feed her tribe. She'd thought of everything. I'd never seen a spread like it. And not a single dish of Chick à la King in sight.

We had a fun evening, made hysterical by a game of charades that had us all doubled over with laughter because David Crosby's response to every song title acted out was, "Penis!"

Around three a.m., we headed home, and some friends passed by us in their car.

"Pandora's Box is re-opening for one night only. We've been invited." They were so excited, and the feeling was contagious. "Stephen Stills has written a song about the riots, and this is going to be the first time he performs it publicly."

Winter grabbed my arm. "We gotta hurry, baby."

As we squeezed into the vehicle, it was evident that half the canyon was heading down to Sunset, everybody excited

96

to hear "For What It's Worth."

"He wrote it in his house in Topanga," Cliff said. "I heard it. It's really cool."

The Los Angeles City Council had condemned Pandora's Box, claiming that it had to be demolished to realign the streets, but for one glorious last hurrah, it was ours again.

No cops came as we quietly filed inside the club. She belonged to the people who loved music and just wanted to hear one of the most talented musicians in the world perform.

I knew practically everyone there. Jack Nicholson made a crack to me. "Waiter, bring me my coffee."

The owner of The 5th Estate and tons of musicians showed up.

"Thank you for being here, and for loving music," Stephen Stills said to the crowd from the tiny stage. We applauded him wildly.

Stephen Stills had to yell over us to be heard. "I wrote my song in about fifteen minutes. For me, there was no riot. It was basically a cop dance."

The crowd went berserk, cheering him on, then he began to play.

"For What it's Worth" was a wonderful song. The chorus brought tears to my eyes and my very soul. We all sang it like a mantra. Over and over again.

It captured a spirit I never could have, even though I was at the revolution. The crowd went mad, then somebody yelled, "Careful, somebody might call the cops!"

That made everyone laugh.

It was hard to leave that place, knowing it would be torn down, but at least I got to go one time and hear a beautiful song.

Outside, Winter said, "How do you want to spend the rest of our Christmas?"

I burst into laughter. "Like I want to spend every other day of the year."

"Is that all you think about, dirty boy?" he asked.

"Yes," I admitted.

He laughed then. "Good thing I do, too."

Up the hill back to the house, we talked about all we were going to do. We spent the night and most of the next day in bed until I had to go to work. This became our routine. We lived only for each other. Only for the times we could be together. He'd stop by my café during the day for coffee, but I knew he wanted to be near me. I'd go to the club at night and watch him work.

We wrote songs together, and soon, other artists wanted to hear them. Even his cousin liked them and started jamming with us, offering to record a demo for us. The song we wrote was called 'Laurel Canyon.' I thought it was pretty cool but still needed some work.

The New Year's Eve bash in Montecito, Santa Barbara was kind of a mess. Something was going on with Jim Morrison.

"He's all over the place like a madman's breakfast," Winter whispered to me between songs. He was in such bad shape we feared he wouldn't want to drive up to Tiburon. We drove right then and there, with Jim sleeping in the back. We reached my old town at four o'clock in the morning.

Poor Brutus seemed older and thinner when I saw him. It broke my heart that my brother had him sleeping in the backyard, and it was so damned cold in Northern California.

"He's got a doghouse," Ray griped. He handed me Brutus' food bowls, leash, and a half-chewed tennis ball.

Jim woke up as we headed home. He was a huge dog lover, and Brutus was, apparently, a huge Jim Morrison fan. They slept all the way home together.

* * * *

The months flew by, and in March, Winter and I were invited to audition for Neil Young, Stephen Stills' bandmate in Buffalo Springfield. We went because we decided if either of us got in the band, it would give our own band a boost. It would be a side project.

I showed up at his house all excited, but not surprised to see a few other guys there, too. It did throw me, however, and my audition wasn't great. Right before me, a strange guy named Charles Manson played. He had the weirdest eyes and manner of anyone I'd ever seen.

"Creepy," Winter said when he ran into him a few days later. "He's heavily into drugs, but I heard he's maybe gonna write some songs with Dennis Wilson.

On August 3rd, John Phillips came down to tell us that Pandora's Box was to be demolished that day. I didn't know if I could stand to watch, but I got ready for work and walked down to Sunset with Winter and Brutus. My beautiful dog had filled out and enjoyed our crazy lifestyle. He and Winter would walk me to work, then stop by friends who had a dog and a pool, then head home again.

We were just in time to see a bunch of suits standing around grinning, and a wrecking ball mowing down the faded but still colorful walls. The traffic still kept moving, and life on the Strip went on, as they turned Pandora's into rubble.

I felt empty afterward. Winter took me in his arms. "There's something I need to tell you."

"What?" I asked as he released me again.

"I'm feeling restless. I want to explore a bit."

The bottom fell out of my world. "Where are you going?"

"A bunch of us want to go to hear Martin Luther King speak. We need to know what's going on in the world. In other parts of the country. It'll be cool. We'll be together."

I stared at him. "You're asking me to go with you?"

"No. I'm *begging* you to come with me."

"I want to go, but..." I wanted to stay. I loved the canyon. I needed the canyon.

"I'm not taking the canyon away from you," he said, as though reading my thoughts. "But music is our life, and we have to feed its soul. We have to seek the inspiration. I'm taking you and Brutus away from Laurel Canyon, but I promise to bring you back to it. Soon."

Letting out the breath I'd been holding my whole life it seemed, I said, "Okay."

"I love you, Taris."

"I love you, too, Winter."

He took my hand, and it really did feel like the Summer of Love. All things were possible, even happiness. I didn't turn to look at the debris of the club that started it all for me. I would be back. And I would sing songs in her memory. And I would love her, and my beloved canyon, deeply, fiercely.

Almost as much as I loved Winter.

"Laurel Canyon wasn't just a music scene; it was a mindset."

Grammy Museum executive director Bob Santelli.

YOU MAY ALSO ENJOY THE FOLLOWING FROM EXTASY BOOKS INC:

Pearls, Porches and Peanuts
A.J. Llewellyn

Excerpt

Dagan Rucker stared across the desk at his agent, Bud Levin.

"It's true," Bud said. "You really inherited a bunch of money."

"From a complete stranger." Dagan couldn't hide his disbelief.

"No. Not a complete. You met her once."

"Once. Oh, that makes us really good friends. Solid. Yeah. Tight. I totally get now why she left me a small fortune." Dagan rolled his eyes.

Bud shrugged. "She saw you as a good friend. According to the terms of her will."

"How do I, er, how did I meet this generous er... fairy godmother?"

"At a book signing."

"Oh, please."

Bud held up a hand. He'd sounded embarrassed when he'd first called two days ago with the news of Dagan's unusual inheritance. He hadn't bothered contacting Dagan once since Cowboy County had been canceled. Well, he'd been canned from the show a year ago, but then the whole thing had blown sky high a few months later. Dagan had retreated to his Topanga Canyon ranch house and converted it to a profitable bed-and-breakfast establishment after he learned his fabulous money manager had embezzled every dime Dagan had ever earned.

I should never have trusted him with everything. I do the same thing with men and get burned at the stake. Frequently. But he'd been smart and leaned on his other asset. Carpentry. Hey, it worked for Jesus. He rented out several bedrooms and had built six cabins and a sturdy bridge over the creek running through his ranch. He'd also brought in a couple of horses. He was booked solid with guests coming nonstop. Some knew who he was, some didn't.

He'd been surprised when Bud called a couple of days ago. Things hadn't gone well between them since Bud had been the one to turn Dagan onto his investment advisor, Mort Blumenstock. Dagan tried to make light of things at first by saying to his friends, "More and that bloomin' stock." One of Jimmy Fallon's show writers overheard him one day and used the gag for Jimmy's speech that night. It was ironic that with a name like that, Blumenstock would turn out to be a crook.

When Mort was arrested, Dagan learned that Bud had already pulled all his accounts, but dozens of his big-name celebrity clients had been cleaned out by the shady financial guru.

There hadn't been much to talk about it, especially when Bud came under the scrutiny of the Department of Justice for removing his accounts from Blumenstock.

Dagan knew that Bud hadn't called these past couple of days with work offers. He would have said so. Dagan cast a critical glance at his former agent, who looked dreadful. Now in his late sixties, Bud's clothes looked dated and worn, and his dark hair needed a cut. An ill-advised scalp surgery in a vain attempt to disguise a huge bald spot on top of his head two few years ago had resulted in the empty space looking about the same, but Bud's eyes now slanted upward and unevenly. He appeared to have had some bad plastic surgery too, giving him an odd look. Was it Botox? Restylane, or whatever they called it? He had smooth patches under one eye and wrinkles under the other. Lumps and strange lines appeared all over the man's face and neck. Dagan wanted to run a gentle iron over them.

He glanced around the office. Unbelievable. The same water stain that had been there the last time Dagan visited was still in the left-hand corner of the ceiling. The drapes were still the same tan colored dust-huggers that made it impossible to tell if it was night or day outside.

The same smell lingered in the air. He sniffed. Old onions, a trace of body odor. And something else. Licorice. That was a surprise.

On Bud's walls were photos of clients. Dagan's was there. So was Tosh Tanner's. Side by side. I'm surprised he didn't chuck those out.

He glanced back at Bud, who was toying with his false teeth with the cap of a ballpoint pen. Honestly. Can't he afford a better fitting set of choppers? Bud had mentioned an attorney's letter. Then came the registered letter sent to the ranch, and a duplicate dispatched to Bud's office. Dagan had ignored Bud's calls and been tempted to blow off the last message he'd left, but now Dagan's dream property was being eaten alive by termites, and one guest had complained of bats flying into her room in the middle of the night.

There was also the matter of the damaged beehives on the ranch. He knew he'd have to wait until dark to repair them. He'd hired a renowned beekeeper to help him, at the hefty price of three grand, but Dagan still had no idea how the entire left side of the units he'd built had been crushed. His thoughts cycled back to the damned bats. He was scared of the cost involved with everything he needed to do, not to mention the long-term harm caused by bad reviews.

"You've inherited money. I checked it out, it's legit," Bud said now. "Look, you can take the money and invest it in Shangri-La or whatever the hell you call it," Bud had said on the phone. "Just come in and talk to me. Please. I have a proposition for you."

And this was how Dagan had left the sanctity of his dusty canyon life and driven east to Santa Monica. It had done him no good heading down the mountain to Pacific Coast Highway. The traffic and noise had gotten to him. The farthest he ever got these days was a straight run down to Malibu's Cross Creek shopping center, where he purchased building supplies he needed at Malibu Lumberyard. He could nip into the gas station and fill up the tank on his pick-up truck, get coffee at The Coffee Bean & Tea Leaf, candles and flowers for his guests from one of the high-end boutiques and the occasional salad from Marmalade Café.

He didn't even go the supermarket these days. His ranch hand, Luis's wife, Marine, who cooked and cleaned for the guests, did the shopping, remembering to slide six-packs of Mountain Dew into the cart for Dagan. His only real vice.

Driving all the way into the business section of Santa Monica hadn't pleased him.

"There's a catch," Bud said.

This made Dagan even less thrilled that he'd made this mad trip. "Of course there is." He blew out a breath. Wasn't there always a catch? The only good things to come out of this excursion were Bud's half-decent coffee and the knowledge that Dagan could get up and walk out any time he liked.

ENDNOTES

The riots depicted in this story are true. I have portrayed them as accurately as possible, thanks to the magic of YouTube videos and online newspaper and radio archives.

The Compton Cafeteria Riot occurred, but the exact date in August 1966 is unknown because not a single newspaper reported it. Old police records were destroyed. However, this largely forgotten event in American history preceded the Stonewall riots by three years and is considered the first real fight for GLBT persons in the U.S.

All of the musicians and actors mentioned were real and have been included in context where possible. All are depicted with love and affection, as is Laurel Canyon.

Pupi's and all the other places existed, and Pupi's owner, Marge Drury, was a real figure, famous for her grumpiness. She took her own life in 1967, and the café closed immediately afterward.

Sadly, movie star Ramon Novarro was murdered in his Laurel Canyon home on the night of October 30, 1968, by two male hustlers who used his lead Art Deco dildo as a weapon.

Musician Frank Zappa eventually took over the famous log cabin depicted here for a brief, frantic summer in 1968. Laurel Canyon legends still abound about some of the activities there. It burned to the ground under mysterious circumstances on Halloween in 1981.

Three songs were written in 1966 that depicted the mood and despair of the Sunset riots. Stephen Stills penned "For What it's Worth" two weeks after the first riot on November

12. Sony Bono (without Cher) recorded a 45 single, "We Have As Much Right to Be Here As Anyone," but I cannot find this song anywhere. Not even on YouTube.

He and Cher really were dropped as MCs of the Rose Parade in January 1967 because of their support of youth rights and the Sunset Riot.

Frank Zappa wrote and recorded "Plastic People" in response to the riot. His lyrics inspired the crazy character of Brent in this story.

My thanks to actor Claudio Martinez for suggesting it.

Barney's Beanery continued to post the abhorrent sign Faggots Stay Out for decades. It was eventually removed when West Hollywood became a formal gay city, on November 29, 1984, the first of its kind in the U.S.

Charles Manson was a well-known figure in Laurel Canyon's music scene. He really did audition for Neil Young, and also for producer Terry Melcher (son of Doris Day). When Melcher failed to sign him to a deal, according to police reports, it was Melcher who was Manson's target for murder the night he dispatched his 'family' to Cielo Drive in Beverly Hills to commit their atrocities.

Melcher had moved, however. They still found innocent targets, and the rest is history.

Manson did write a song with Dennis Wilson, and The Beach Boys recorded it. 'Never Learn Not to Love' was released in 1968. When Manson discovered that The Beach Boys hadn't given him a writing credit, he threatened to kill Dennis Wilson. He went to his house, but Wilson beat him up. Shortly after this, the Manson murders took place, and Wilson became rightfully paranoid.

No sign of the triangle occupied by Pandora's Box remains today. It was eliminated by the Los Angeles city street rerouting. Today the corner is home to a McDonald's restaurant, a Chase bank branch, and a storage facility in a mall called Sunset Plaza that was built in 2000.

It is nothing like the magnificent Garden of Allah, the lush property created by the silent screen star Alla Nazimova that once stood there, long before Pandora's Box was built.

Smog, traffic, and water are still big issues in California. Though so many places depicted in this story have disappeared, some things stay the same.

Winter and Taris lived happily ever after. And still, do.

The fight for GLBTQ rights continues all over the world. Let's love each other, regardless of race, color, creed, or sexual orientation.

It's time we stop, hey, what's that sound?

With Love,
A.J.

ABOUT THE AUTHOR

A.J. Llewellyn is the author of over 250 M/M romance novels. She was born in Australia, and lives in Los Angeles. An early obsession with Robinson Crusoe led to a lifelong love affair with islands, particularly Hawaii and Easter Island.

Being marooned once on Wedding Cake Island in Australia cured her of a passion for fishing, but led to a plotline for a novel. A.J.'s friends live in fear because even the smallest details of their lives usually wind up in her stories. A.J. has a desire to paint, draw, juggle, work for the FBI, walk a tightrope with an elephant, be a chess champion, a steeplejack, master chef, and a world-class surfer. She can't do any of these things so she writes about them instead.

A.J. started life as a journalist and boxing columnist, and still enjoys interrogating, er, interviewing people to find out what makes them tick.

How to find/friend me:

email: ajllewellyn@gmail.com
website: www.ajllewellyn.com
www.facebook.com/aj.llewellyn
www.twitter.com/ajllewellyn
Newsletter sign-up: ajllewellynnewsletter@gmail.com—each month I give away a free ebook!
I'm an app! Download my FREE A.J. Llewellyn App for Android here: http://tinyurl.com/lkbc4wm

www.ingramcontent.com/pod-product-compliance
Lightning Source LLC
Chambersburg PA
CBHW070455130626
46555CB00003B/1011